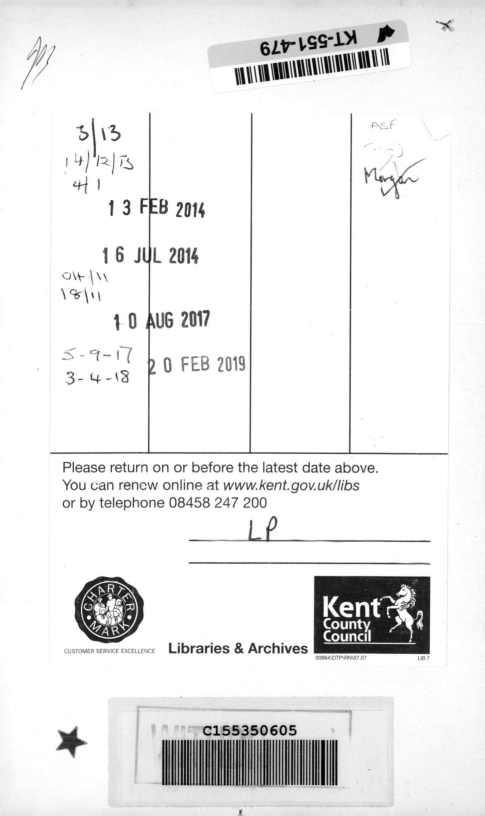

# THE BAKER'S DAUGHTER

Anne Forsyth

**CHIVERS**

British Library Cataloguing in Publication Data available

This Large Print edition published by AudioGO Ltd, Bath, 2012.
Published by arrangement with the Author

U.K. Hardcover   ISBN  978 1 4458 4640 8
U.K. Softcover   ISBN  978 1 4458 4641 5

Printed and bound in Great Britain by
MPG Books Group Limited

# 'SHE TOLD ME TO GO'

*'Ma feet's cauld, ma shoes thin, Gie us oor cakes an' let us rin.'* Two or three children crowded around the front door of Maclaren's Quality Baker's, chanting in a ragged chorus.

Angus Maclaren, owner of the shop, turned from rearranging the display of tins of shortbread and shook his head.

'I thought they'd given up that caper a year or two back.'

'You're going to send them away, I hope?' The woman behind the till was scrawny, dressed in black, her spectacles on the end of her nose. You would not have guessed that Lizzie Maclaren had ever been a child, let alone a bairn like those clustered hopefully around the door.

'Och, Lizzie,' said the baker. 'It's an old Scots tradition every ne'erday.'

She sniffed. 'More an excuse for begging, if you ask me.' Her brother paid no attention and brought from the back premises a large brown paper bag.

'There you are.' He handed it to the tallest of the children. 'Now that's all there is, so you can tell any more of your pals not to bother coming to the door.'

'Thanks, mister!' The children fell gleefully on the bag of yesterday's cakes and cookies,

1

sharing them out, before they ran off, whooping and screeching and fighting for the privilege of bursting the paper bag.

'They're just a nuisance, those bairns.' Lizzie paused in adding up a column of figures. 'Bairns will take advantage if you let them away with things. Ruby was too soft with them.'

'I'll thank you not to be criticising Ruby.'

Lizzie recognised the tone of voice and said no more. She knew by now that her brother wouldn't stand for any criticism of his Ruby.

Poor Ruby, she thought, if she'd lived . . . Angus had been a lost soul without her—*and what would he have done*, Lizzie told herself, with a sudden spurt of anger.

*How would he have looked after those motherless bairns, if I hadn't come to the rescue?*

Angus Maclaren finished rearranging the display. She was a good soul at heart, was his sister, but she could be very trying. Still, he thought, she had a grand head for figures and she ran his home efficiently. If only she had a bit more humour about her . . .

But now it was Hogmanay, and who knew what 1952 would bring.

'So what'll it be today, Mrs Maclean?' he greeted the customer who pushed open the glass door.

'An awful day, this,' she said, unwinding the shawl she had tied round her head. 'My, it's a dreary start to the New Year and that's a fact.'

2

Angus asked politely about her state of health—it was his custom to do this before they got on to the topic of pan loaves, soda scones or fruit cake and the like.

'I'll not see the year out,' she returned gloomily. 'Aye, who knows what'll happen this year?'

Angus thought briefly of the country—those long years of war and austerity, but at last things seemed to be taking a turn for the better.

No coupons for bread any more—those dreaded bread units and long queues. Angus had always refused to keep cakes under the counter. 'First come, first served,' he'd said firmly. 'So what is the matter?' he asked his customer with a sigh.

'It's my feet. I'm a martyr to my feet.'

'Take a seat,' he invited her, drawing forward a chair in front of the counter.

'Thank you kindly.' She plumped herself down on the chair.

'I saw your lassie,' Mrs Maclean continued. 'The other evening—with a boy.' Her voice dropped as she imparted this information. 'The Tulloch boy . . .'

'Oh, yes?' Angus said.

'Just so.' Mrs Maclean was a little disappointed that the baker didn't seem to be disturbed by her piece of news. She added, 'All dressed up, she was.' She drew in her breath.

Angus coughed. He made up his mind to

have a word with Rona when she appeared.

The Tulloch boy had a bit of a reputation for being wild. 'Rona's twenty,' he said. 'Old enough to go out with boys.'

'You need to watch,' said Mrs Maclean. 'Lassies—they're all the same. You want to see she doesn't get into trouble. She wouldn't be the first and she wouldn't be the last.'

If only, he thought, this customer would take her custom to another baker's, but Maclaren's was known to be the best in the town.

'So what'll it be?'

'I'll take a pan loaf and half a dozen treacle scones.'

When at last she heaved herself out of the chair, Angus opened the door for her. 'A good New Year to you, Mrs Maclean, when it comes.'

'Ah, well,' she said gloomily 'We'll just need to take what's sent to us. What's for us will no gae past us.'

'Just so.' Angus closed the door on her and turned to face his sister.

'Did you hear that?'

'What?' He busied himself making up the order for the hotel. Dundee cake, shortbread, black bun . . .

'What she said, that woman, about your Rona. And a boy . . .'

'Yes, I heard.'

'So what are you going to do about it?' she

demanded.

'Leave it to me. I'll have a word.'

'And so you should. That laddie's been in trouble with the police.'

'I said, leave it to me. I'll speak to her.'

'Make sure you do.' She turned back to checking the invoices. From then on, the shop was busy with customers, buying tins of shortbread, black bun and fruit cakes.

Angus thought, as he wrapped tins, and boxed fancy cakes, that it was time he had an assistant. But who was there?

Lots of the lads in the town were still away on National Service—and not many wanted to work in a baker's. Like his own lad, Doug, who had worked in the garage since he left school. Not that Doug was a problem—the problem was Rona.

'A good New Year to you!' He closed the door behind the last customer and pulled down the blinds. 'That's us, then. As soon as I've swept up and cleaned the shop I'll get away. Why don't you go? You'll have things to do at home.'

'I might at that . . .'

They were interrupted by a knock on the door.

'We're closed,' Angus began, but reluctant to turn away a customer, he unlocked the door.

'Rona! I didn't expect you.'

The girl who stood on the shop doorstep

5

was tall and slim with untidy gold hair. In the cold December air, her cheeks were flushed and her eyes sparkled.

'I thought I'd come and surprise you. Old Mrs Fowler let me off early . . .' She made a face. As a companion to the old lady at the big house just beyond the little town of Kirkton, Rona was a sore trial to the grim housekeeper who liked everything done by the book.

Oh, dear, thought Rona, looking round the shop. It never changed. It had been the same always since she was a small girl. There was Father, in his white overall behind the counter, and Aunt Lizzie—Rona thought she looked like a black crow in a cage, sitting at the cash desk . . .

She grinned to herself. And the tins, neatly stacked, the counter, scrubbed every night. Who would want to work here, year in, year out?

'Well, this is a surprise!' Angus smiled at his daughter. 'I was just clearing up. And your aunt's on the way home.'

Lizzie put on her hat and adjusted it in front of the mirror that advertised a well known brand of sugar biscuits.

'If that's all right with you . . .' she hesitated. 'I've things to do for the morn.'

'Away you go,' said Angus.

'I'll help you clear up,' Rona offered. 'Tell me what to do.'

'You'll need to clear the window display

6

then wipe the shelves.'

Window display, thought Rona. The same tins of shortbread had been there for years.

'Right you are.'

Angus kept an eye on what she was doing. Rona was slapdash, he knew that. She was of little real use. How long she would last at any job, he often thought to himself, was in doubt. And yet, he told himself, as she went energetically about her task; humming tunefully, *Singing in the Rain*, she was a happy presence to have around.

He paused. Was this the time to talk to her about the Tulloch boy?

'Rona?'

'Yes?' She was wringing out the cloth and hanging it up to dry.

'Are you, er, going out tonight?'

'It's Hogmanay, Father.'

'Well, I just thought, you might perhaps be going out with . . .' he paused. 'Your friends.'

She stood, glaring at him. 'I know fine what you're on about,' she said angrily. 'It's that old cat, Mrs Maclean, isn't it? The biggest and worst gossip in Kirkton.'

'Well,' said Angus as mildly as he could, 'she did mention something.'

'That she'd seen me with a boy.'

'Well, yes.'

'So?'

'You're far too young,' said Angus more firmly. 'Too young to be running around with

7

boys. Especially the Tulloch lad.'

'I'm grown up, Father,' she said, exasperated.

Suddenly a thought struck Angus.

'Should you not be still at your work?'

Rona hesitated. 'I got away early.'

Angus paused, and carefully replaced a tin on the shelf. He turned to face his daughter.

'So?'

She didn't meet his gaze. 'So?' she mimicked.

'Don't you give me that, young lady,' said Angus sharply. 'I'll not have your impertinence. Why are you not at your work?'

Rona sighed. 'If you must know . . .'

'I'm waiting.'

'Well, I've resigned.'

'You've what?'

'I said . . .' she looked sulky. 'I've left. It wasn't my fault—that old cat, Mrs Jackson, the housekeeper—she'd got it in for me. I only broke a vase,' she said defensively. 'But she cast it up to me—and all the other things I was supposed to have done. Well,' she swept back her hair. 'I wasn't having that. So I told her I was leaving.'

'The truth,' said Angus grimly.

'She told me to go,' said Rona in a small voice.

'So you got the sack.'

'Well . . .'

'You had a good place there,' said her

8

father coldly. 'You could have stayed there, learned a lot.'

'I didn't like it,' said Rona. 'I'd never liked it.'

'It was a job.' Her father spaced out the words. 'Jobs are hard to get. You've no training . . .'

'The teachers said I could go on to college. Maybe.'

'Aye, if you got a bursary. But where's the money to come from? And you wouldn't stick in. You never have.'

They stood silent, glaring at each other.

Angus went on, 'You've been in that many jobs. The chemist's—that didn't last, nor the wool shop. It's not that there aren't jobs to be had. You've only to look at the Fife News— there're adverts, folk looking for girls to work at the hospital, Farm Mec are wanting office girls to train, and there're jobs going at the printers in Cupar. You can learn shorthand and typing.'

He paused. 'But no-one's wanting a girl that's been sacked that many times.' He gave an exasperated sigh. 'So what do you want to do?'

'I want to be a model,' said Rona defiantly.

'Save us!' Angus roared, his patience at an end. 'A model!' Thank goodness, he thought, that her Aunt Lizzie had gone home and wasn't here to listen to this nonsense. 'And what makes you think you could be a model?'

'I'd like to go to London,' Rona said. 'There's others get modelling jobs, and I'm just as good as them. You can earn a lot of money,' she added hopefully.

'Well, you can put that out of your mind for a start,' said Angus. 'I never heard anything like it.'

He paused. 'Ah, well,' said Angus at last, 'what's done can't be undone. There's only one thing for it. I'll take you on here,' he decided.

'But . . .' Rona began.

'No buts. I want you here where I can keep an eye on you. You can start by sweeping the floor. You'll find the brush and dustpan behind the door And,' he added, 'I want to hear no more about you running around with boys. Is that clear?'

'It was only . . .'

'That lad has a bad reputation. You'll do as I say.'

He sighed. What was he to do with this wayward daughter? Ruby would have known how to handle her. Lizzie—well, she was of no help at all.

She and Rona were constantly at war, and it made for an uneasy atmosphere in the home. 'At your age,' Lizzie would say, pursing her lips, 'I did what my elders and betters told me.'

'But,' Rona would argue, 'we're in the nineteen fifties now. Not the Dark Ages,' she would add under her breath.

I'll maybe regret this, thought Angus.

10

Taking her on in the shop. She's that headstrong. And there was bound to be trouble with Lizzie. If only . . . But there was no use regretting. And to be fair, Rona hadn't really had a chance, what with her mother dying when she was just about to leave school.

It was not, he thought, going to be the cheeriest Hogmanay he'd ever had. Doug—well, he was old enough by now. He'd want to be out with his friends. Rona—he shuddered—would resent staying at home.

But then, he recalled, there would be friends dropping in. There would be a first foot—someone tall, and dark. It was nearly always Geordie from next door. He'd bring his accordion, and someone would sing, or give a comic recitation. And there would be black bun—he thought proudly of the black bun that was his speciality, dark, rich and spicy, and a dram to welcome in 1952. Oh, it might not be too bad after all.

He thought back to the dark years of the war. Everything in short supply, no sugar for iced cakes, and queues all along the street.

He remembered, you couldn't even provide a wedding cake. Lots of brides had to make do with a cardboard cake—and when you took off the top layer inside was a wee bit of sponge.

It was even worse after the war, just when bread was rationed—1948, he remembered, before the two years of bread rationing ended.

How tired he had been of these dreaded

coupons—bread units, BUs they called them. But now things were beginning to improve.

Oh, there were some shortages still, but gradually life was getting back to normal, though it had been a long slow business, and rationing wasn't ended yet.

It would be grand, he thought, to return to producing the elaborate cream cakes of pre-war—though he had to admit, the mock cream that had filled cream horns hadn't been all that bad, made with margarine, sugar and dried milk powder.

He'd done his best this year to provide something extra for Christmas and Hogmanay, such as the old folks' boxes he'd made up with gingerbread, a piece of sultana cake and shortbread. They'd sold well at eight shillings a box—there were none left.

Just as he was about to close up, there was a sound outside. *'Ma feet's cauld, ma shoes are thin . . .'*

He sighed, exasperated. 'I've already given these bairns their Hogmanay.'

But there were scones and some tea bread left—they'd be stale by the time the shop opened again.

He reached for a bag and filled it, then opened the door. 'Now that's the last—there's no more. So you needn't be telling any of your pals to come round.'

The biggest boy in the group grabbed the bag with a whoop of joy. 'Thanks, mister.'

The rest of them crowded round to see what treasures they'd been given.

'Thanks, mister. A good New Year to you when it comes.'

Angus smiled 'And a good New Year to you,' he said, as he closed the door.

Rona grimaced. Would it really be a good New Year? Oh, it was dull in Kirkton, and it promised to be even drearier working in the shop under the watchful eye of Aunt Lizzie.

If only . . . she wished she could leave, find a job in the city, Edinburgh or Glasgow or even London. She had never been to London. But then she began to cheer up. Rona was seldom down in spirits for long.

There had been a boy last week at the dance in the town hall who had whirled her round in a quickstep and told her she was the prettiest girl there. And another—he was rather boring, she had to admit—who had asked her to go to the pictures.

Still, this was the beginning of a new year— and who knew what might happen? Maybe, she told herself, romance was just around the corner.

## BORED IN THE SHOP

'I hate this job,' said Rona to herself. 'Out of the frying pan into the fire.' She wished sometimes that she hadn't been quite so impulsive, that she'd tried harder to fit into the job at the big house. 'At least,' she reminded herself, 'I wasn't working for Father.'

It was even worse being in the shop with Aunt Lizzie the whole time. She thought of the conversation she'd had with her friend, Nancy, the previous evening.

'Do you like that colour?' Nancy had said, examining the bright scarlet she'd painted her nails.

'My father would have a fit if I painted my nails that colour,' said Rona gloomily.

'You should stand up for yourself.' Nancy shook her dark curls. 'There—I've smudged a nail,' she said in exasperation. 'You could easily be a model,' she went on.

'Do you think so?'

'You've got the height,' said Nancy earnestly.

'I've seen these models,' said Rona thoughtfully, 'in the big stores—that time we went to Edinburgh. They walk through the tearoom holding a card with the price. I could easily do that.'

She jumped up and pretended to be a model swaying her way through the tea tables with a haughty expression.

Nancy fell back, laughing. 'There you are. You're perfect!'

'But I'll never get the chance,' said Rona gloomily. 'My father thinks I'm no good at

14

anything—but I can add up, and I'd really like a chance to do the windows. They've looked the same for donkeys' years.'

She turned to her friend. 'Look at your family,' she said. 'They let you leave school, and there you are working in the council offices.'

'Just till the right man comes along,' said Nancy, 'and then I'm off.' She spent many of the hours at work day dreaming about the perfect wedding dress.

'Oh, you,' scoffed Rona who hadn't given a thought to weddings. Unless it was as the bride at the end of a fashion show, making her way slowly along the catwalk.

'Ooh, isn't she lovely?' She could hear the applause of the audience and graciously looked from left to right before she turned with a sweep of the long silk train . . .

\*       \*       \*

'A real family business,' said an old lady as she paid for a brown loaf and some potato scones.

Rona overheard her and glared. Luckily the old woman was exchanging news with Aunt Lizzie, and didn't see, but Rona earned a ticking-off from Angus. 'The customer is always right,' he said sternly. 'How often do I have to tell you?'

But most of the time, Angus was in a good mood. Business was brisk and he felt he could

15

invest in a new van.

'It's necessary—for the deliveries,' he excused himself. 'I could never be sure that the old one wouldn't break down—and me maybe miles away delivering to a farm somewhere.'

Because for him it was a matter of pride— early deliveries, morning rolls and bread, later in the day, tea bread and cakes.

'There you are.' He gestured proudly towards the van, with its gilt lettering, *Maclaren—Family Baker*.

Rona felt more dispirited than ever. Maclaren's would go on for ever and ever. The fact that the lettering proclaimed it in gilt words made it all the more certain. She had only worked in the shop for a couple of weeks, and oh, she was bored.

'Can I get a shot?' Doug was round immediately to see the new van.

'That you cannot.' Angus was firm. 'No-one gets to drive this van but me?'

'I can drive, Father, honest I can. Sanny lets me drive the cars in the garage.'

'What he does is his own business,' said Angus solemnly. 'This is a working vehicle not for you to run around in with your pals.'

Doug sighed. There was no moving Father when he was like this. He shrugged his shoulders and turned to go back to the garage where the doctor's new Ford Consul was in for a service. Now there was a car—leather upholstery, heater and all.

16

'I'd quite like to have a go,' said Rona who had come out to the front and stood admiring the van.

She was supposed to be making up orders, but this was much more interesting. She wiped her hands on her white apron—the apron that had been white that morning—and brushed back a few tendrils of hair.

'Have a go, you will not,' said Angus severely. 'I've told you, no-one drives this van but me.' He ran a hand lovingly over the shining bonnet then turned to chase away a crowd of children who had gathered.

'Give us a hurl in it, mister! Go on . . .'

Angus ignored them. He turned back to Rona. 'Away and sort out the delivery for the hotel,' he told her.

Sulking, Rona did as she was told.


## 'YOU'RE NO CREDIT TO THE FAMILY'

Later that day, the door opened and Rona tried not to stare at the elegant figure who stopped and gazed around the shop. 'I'm looking for something really special,' she said in a languid drawl.

'English,' said Rona to herself 'Not from around here anyway.'

She took in the customer's dress, figured in a geometric print, and her little black velvet

17

hat with a veil, perched at a fetching angle on her dark hair.

'You'll find something special here, madam,' said Rona in her best saleswoman's voice. Behind her, at the desk, she could hear Aunt Lizzie sniff. Whether it was disapproval of Rona's manner, or whether she was inhaling the musk of the visitor's perfume that wafted round the shop—it was hard to tell. Rona paid no attention.

'Would it be for afternoon tea?' she continued.

'I'd like some of your fruit cake.'

'None better,' said Rona.

'I'm sure.' The woman looked rather coldly at Rona. 'What else? Scones?'

'Freshly baked today,' said Rona.

'Very well, I'll take half a dozen. What besides?' She looked rather vaguely along the display of potato scones, pancakes and soda scones.

Immediately Rona recognised someone who wasn't accustomed to shopping for herself, and set about selling enthusiastically.

'We've some nice apple tarts,' she said. 'A speciality of our shop,' she added grandly.

'I'll take a dozen.'

'Right you are,' said Rona forgetting in her enthusiasm to be the sophisticated sales lady. 'They're in the back shop, newly baked. I'll just get a tray.'

The customer leaned against the counter,

inspecting her fingernails in a bored sort of way.

But as Rona emerged from the back of the shop, the front door burst open, blown by a gust of wind and a small black Pekinese, dragging its lead, bounded into the shop, yapping angrily.

'Toots, you are naughty,' the customer exclaimed. 'I told you to wait outside.'

'Here you are . . .' Rona began, just as the dog rushed towards her. She tripped over the lead and her tray of apple tarts went flying and she crashed to the floor.

Aunt Lizzie rose from the cash desk. 'Get up, Rona,' she said crossly.

Rona, mortified, rose to her feet, rubbing her elbow where she had hit it against the edge of the counter.

The dog, meantime, had gobbled up one apple tart and was starting on a second.

'Oh, poor little thing,' the customer swept the dog into her arms. 'Are you all right?'

'Yes, thank you,' said Rona before she realised that the customer was addressing the Pekinese.

She looked gloomily at the tray of apple tarts now spread all over the floor.

'Will that be all, madam?' she said with as much dignity as she could.

'Dear me,' said the customer, looking disdainfully at the floor. Her gaze swept the Shop. 'Is this the only baker's in the town?' she said.

'There is another,' said. Rona, 'but this is the best.'

'Really?' The lady's tone was chilly 'Is it?' Her attention was drawn to her little dog, licking the floor happily 'Oh, sweetie, don't do that. It may not even be clean.'

Aunt Lizzie now entered the conversation. 'Can we be of further assistance to you, madam?'

The customer shook her head. 'How much is that now?' She produced her purse from her dainty black pochette, and said to Rona, 'That will be all.'

Rona wrapped up the items she'd bought and put them into a box.

When the customer had paid and taken herself and her dog away, Rona looked at the floor with dismay.

'You'd best get that all cleaned up,' said Aunt Lizzie behind her. 'Before your father comes back. I never saw the like of it. If there's a wrong thing to do, you'll do it.

'Yesterday you dropped these cream cookies, and you forgot the order for potato scones.' She said grimly, 'You're no help to your father, none at all. You can't be left for a minute.'

'I'm doing my best,' Rona defended herself.

'Aye, well. I'm not surprised they gave you your books from the big house.'

'It's always the same.' Rona flared up.

20

'Whatever I do, it's the wrong thing. There's no pleasing you, ever!'

'You'll not speak to me like that, miss. I'm not having it.' Aunt Lizzie's cheeks flushed.

'Well,' said Rona, nearly in tears. 'I don't want to work here.'

'And what are you fit for, may I ask?' her aunt said grimly. 'There's precious few places would employ you, and you so handless. It's not as if you were any help in the house—mind that time you scorched your father's best shirt, supposed to be ironing it.'

'That was a while ago!' Rona said angrily 'And you're never done casting it up to me.'

'Well, all I can say is, you're no credit to the family and no help to your father, poor soul.'

At this reference to her father, Rona had had enough and she burst into tears.

She wiped her eyes with a corner of her apron and went into the back shop to fetch the brush and pan.

Just then the door opened. A customer, thought Rona, with a gulp, and the shop in a proper state.

She turned to greet the person who had entered, and saw a stocky, fair-haired young man with a cheerful expression. He looked a little dismayed as he looked at the floor.

'Oh, sorry. I've come at a bad time.'

'Not at all,' said Rona, with a sniff. She put away her handkerchief. 'What can I get you?'

'I came in for a pie for my piece,' he said,

but . . .'

'It's all right,' Rona tried to sound normal. 'I just dropped a tray of apple tarts.'

He walked cautiously through towards the counter. 'The floor's a bit sticky,' he said.

'I was just going to clean it up,' said Rona.

'I'll give you a hand. Can't have the customers tramping apple tarts into the floor, can we? Have you got a mop and a pail?'

'In the back shop.'

'Right you are.' He nodded pleasantly to Aunt Lizzie.

As Rona swept up the crumbled remains of the tarts, he filled the pail with soapy water, and began to mop.

'There's one here not broken,' he said. 'Could I have it?'

'I wouldn't,' said Rona solemnly. 'The last person—the woman they were meant for—she had a dog with her, and it ate up one or two. I can't think why it left that one. So it's probably not very clean.'

'Pity,' said the young man. 'I rather like apple tarts.'

'It's very kind of you to help my niece,' said Aunt Lizzie from her position at the cash desk. 'I would myself, but my legs . . .'

'It's no trouble at all,' he said politely. 'There you are. That's better.' He stood back and looked at the floor. 'Maybe we'd best open the door till it dries out.'

'It's very kind of you,' said Rona, suddenly

22

shy. 'I don't know what I would have done . . . if it had been another customer wanting bread or something.'

'Or apple tarts,' he agreed. 'Speaking of which, I don't suppose there are any more?'

'Sorry,' said Rona. 'It was a whole tray—and that's the last of them.'

'I'll need to come back tomorrow then.' He smiled at her, a cheerful impudent sort of grin.

'You wanted a pie,' Rona reminded him.

'So I did.'

'We've pork and bean pies,' said Rona. 'They're nice.'

'That'll do me.'

Rona put the pie into a paper bag.

'How much is that?'

'Nothing,' said Rona. 'You have that—with our compliments—as a thank you, for your help.'

'My, that's good of you.' He grinned again. 'It'll taste extra special. I'll be on my way then?'

'Well, that looks a bit better,' said Aunt Lizzie with approval. 'A nice helpful lad—but you've no call to be giving away pies. You'll have us all in the poorhouse.'

Rona paid no attention. Who was he? She wondered. She hadn't seen him in the town.

Maybe he was new here. Would she see him again? Would he really come back tomorrow?

# A NEW FRIEND

For a few days, Rona wondered about the young man. But then again she was so busy in the shop that she hardly had any time for thought.

There were orders to be made up, shelves to be cleaned, new supplies to be checked, and Father was out twice a day in the new van delivering to farms and the outlying areas.

By the time it came to shut up shop, Rona was exhausted.

\*     \*     \*

One evening about a week later, as she made her way along the street, someone called to her.

'Hello! Any more apple tarts?'

She whirled round The young man with the fair hair was waiting at the corner. He grinned at her.

'Sorry—I shouldn't tease you.'

Rona smiled forgivingly. 'Not at all—you were a great help!'

'I meant to come back to the shop, but we've been a bit busy. I haven't really had a day off. And,' he said, 'to be honest, I'm a bit scared of your aunt.'

'Me, too.'

They both laughed.

'My name's Callum—Callum Scott. And you?' he said enquiringly.

'Rona—Rona Maclaren. My father owns the shop.'

'Have you always worked there?'

She hesitated. 'Just since I left—well, was asked to leave my last job.'

'How do you like working for your father?'

'Not much,' she said frankly. 'Well, he's all right, but Aunt Lizzie . . . I've lots of ideas, for window displays and so on, but she won't let me.'

'Shame that. I work for my father too—at Harefield Farm.'

'I know it.'

There was a pause. 'It's my half day,' he said, 'so I'm in the town getting a few things from the ironmonger.' He added, a little shyly, 'I was hoping I might bump into you.'

Rona smiled back at him. But then she was distracted—by the sight of a car parked at the corner.

She recognised the young man helping the girl into the passenger seat. For a moment, her attention was focused on the girl, short black hair, scarlet lipstick and a bright yellow frilly blouse and skirt.

She looked like someone from another world than the sober, everyday world of Kirkton. Rona found herself staring—who could she be?

There was no doubt about the young man who was helping her into the car with such concern.

'Hello!' she called. 'Doug?'

Her brother turned briefly and saw her, but he ignored her, ducked into the car, and drove off along the street.

'I'd better go for my bus,' said Callum.

'Oh, yes?' she turned towards him. 'Sorry . . .'

'Was that someone you know?'

'My brother,' said Rona a little grimly.

'So I'll see you around. I'll come into the shop next time I'm into the town. If I can brave your aunt.'

'Yes, do.' But Rona was only half paying attention as he waved and went off down the street.

Who was the girl? Where had Doug found her? And why was he so anxious to avoid a meeting?


## ROMANCE FOR DOUG

'Pass the potatoes to your father,' Aunt Lizzie told Rona. The atmosphere that evening was strained.

Rona wondered how much her aunt had told Angus about the disaster a few days earlier.

26

He knew, of course, about the apple tarts and told Rona to be more careful in future, but did he know that the customer had said she'd go to another baker in future? To Keith's, possibly—the other baker was in a more central position, right on the town square.

Their scones, thought Rona loyally, were nothing like as good as Maclaren's, but they did a good trade in birthday cakes and special occasion cakes.

She'd passed one day and noticed a large birthday cake in the window, with pink icing that bore the legend, *The Best Gran In The World.*

Angus had sniffed when she told him about it. 'We'll have nothing of that sort here,' he'd said sternly.

A pity, thought Rona. People would continue to go to Keith's for anything a bit out of the ordinary. Whereas everyone knew that Maclaren's black bun and shortbread were the best in the district.

But now Angus sat thoughtfully. Rona glanced at Doug who avoided her gaze. Who had he been seeing? Why was he so secretive?

After the meal she helped Aunt Lizzie to clear up, and then went through to the living room where her father was reading the evening paper.

'Ah, well, I'm away out.' Doug had been standing looking out of the window, his hands in his pockets.

Angus looked up from the paper. 'You're out most nights,' he said mildly.

'Ah, well . . .' Doug shifted from one foot to the other. 'I've friends to see.'

Angus said no more, but Rona, carrying a tray, stopped Doug in the passage towards the scullery.

'Who are you seeing, then?' she asked.

'None of your business.'

'Is it that girl?'

'I told you,' he said sharply. 'It's nothing to do with you who I see.'

'I saw you with that girl,' Rona persisted. 'What's her name?'

Doug glared at her. 'I told you. It's not your business. And,' he added, changing tack, 'if you go telling Father, I'll . . .'

'I wouldn't.' Rona was hurt. 'I'm not a clype. I don't go telling tales on folk.'

'Well, see you don't.'

'You should bring her home for her tea,' she called after him, teasingly.

He ignored her, and she felt a bit ashamed. It wasn't her business who he saw, and anyway, she grinned, she could just see Aunt Lizzie's face when confronted with the girl with her thick make-up and scarlet nails.

She turned back to the sitting room where Aunt Lizzie had started work on an embroidered runner for a dressing table. Angus was reading items out of the newspaper.

28

'Is there anything about Princess Elizabeth?' Aunt Lizzie asked.

'The tour of Kenya?'

'Aye.'

'Just a picture of the King waving them off on the plane.'

'Let me see.' Aunt Lizzie put down the silks she had chosen. She scanned the paper, and handed it back. There was silence as she began to stitch.

*       *       *

'They know about you,' said Doug glumly, that evening. Neela raised her pencil-thin eyebrows.

'And why not?' she said. 'You're not ashamed of me, are you?' She tucked her hand into the crook of his arm.

'No, of course not,' he said hastily. 'It's just that—well, you know how people talk.'

'There's nothing to talk about,' she said sharply.

'Nothing at all,' he said, but he still couldn't forget that exchange with Rona earlier in the evening.

His mind went back to his meeting with Neela—what was it, two months ago now?

He'd first met her when he went to a local dance in the town hall. She had been leaning against the wall, not at all embarrassed to be on her own, smoking a cigarette in a long

29

scarlet holder. Among the local girls she looked like an exotic flower.

Doug had never seen anyone like her. Her beautifully groomed hair, the vivid red lips, her general air of sophistication—what was she doing here?

'I dare you to ask that one to dance.' His friend, Fred, jerked his head towards the corner where Neela had stood coolly watching the dancers.

Doug had laughed. 'She'd never look at me.'

'Go on.'

They teased Doug a good deal at the garage. Some of the others were courting— nice sensible girls who were saving for their bottom drawer. But who was this girl, and where had she come from?

'All right,' he said suddenly.

'They'd slapped him on the back. 'Good old Doug. Well done.'

Doug had stammered out his invitation to dance. And she'd smiled at him—he did hope his friends were watching.

'I'm not much of a dancer,' he said apologetically as he had trodden for the third time on the black suede shoes.

She made a face. 'No, you're not, are you? But you've won your bet.'

His face flamed.

'I know,' she said calmly, 'your friends were daring you to dance with me.'

'No, well, yes. I mean . . .' he stammered.

'Never mind,' she said. 'Come on, let's sit this one out and you can buy me a lemonade.'

Up in the gallery, looking down on the dancers, she turned to him.

'So what's your name?'

'I'm Doug Maclaren.'

'And what do you do, Doug?'

'I'm . . .' Doug hesitated. He was only an apprentice in the garage, though the boss, Sanny Munro, had said he was doing well, and he expected to be promoted to mechanic.

'I'm in cars,' he said.

'Ooh . . .' she sounded impressed. 'So when you take a girl out, you've got a smashing new Bentley, or an MG, maybe?' She gave him a roguish sideways look.

'And you?' he said. 'I've not seen you around,' he said. 'Are you new to the town?'

She paused. 'Not exactly. I've been working in Edinburgh, but it didn't suit me. I've come back for a bit while I look round.'

'So, are you working round here?'

'For a bit,' she said casually. 'Till I find something else in the city.' She added, 'I'm the sort of girl who likes the bright lights—cafés, theatres, dance halls. Real dance halls, I mean. Not,' she glanced down at the dancers, 'not somewhere like this.'

'So you don't stay in the town?'

'My, you ask a lot of questions.' She nudged his arm.

'Cheeky, eh? Well, I'm staying at home

31

meantime, just till I decide what to do. It's a one-horse town.' She attempted an American accent, not very successfully, but Doug was impressed.

'Then,' said Doug, greatly daring, 'maybe we could go out one evening, to the pictures? Do you like the pictures?'

'Eh,' she said, 'you're a fast worker, aren't you, Doug? But mind you, I like a lad with a bit of go in him.'

Doug said bashfully, 'Well, whatever you like. What about the pictures?'

'If there's a Cary Grant film,' she said dreamily. 'He's my favourite—so sophisticated.'

Doug decided to lose no time. 'How about Friday evening?' he said. 'About six. I'll pick you up.'

'No,' she said, a little too quickly. 'Better if I meet you in the town. Outside the Regal at six p.m., and don't keep me waiting.'

'Oh, I'll not do that.'

'And I hope it's a good film. I like a romance.'

She turned her smile on him, and Doug was hooked. He had to get to know this girl—she was unlike anyone he had met before.

# SPENDING TIME WITH CALLUM

When they met that Friday evening outside the Regal, Doug was very nervous. He had just enough money for the front of the circle, and he'd bought a small box of mint creams.

He was there a good quarter-of-an-hour before. Would she be there as she had promised? Or had she thought better of it?

But a few minutes after six, she arrived. If anything she looked even more glamorous—in a bright red coat, and black high-heeled shoes.

'Did you think I wasn't coming?' she said 'Sorry I'm a bit late. I got held up at the . . .'

She bit the words back, but Doug was so entranced by her that he didn't notice.

'I've got the tickets,' he said. 'And there's a wee box of sweeties for you.'

'Oh, I like a generous man,' she smiled at him 'So what's the big picture?'

'I know you said you liked Cary Grant, but the film's not on till next week.'

'Oh, well, as you've bought the tickets, we might as well use them.'

Doug knew from then on, that the evening was not going well. She wouldn't let him hold her hand during the film, and she refused an ice-cream in the interval, though she ate most of the box of mints.

As the audience streamed out of the

33

cinema, she turned to him. 'Thanks, Doug.'

Doug said desperately, 'Have you not time for a coffee?' He himself would have liked a cup of tea, but he thought coffee sounded more sophisticated.

'Not tonight,' she said quickly. 'I'd better be getting back.'

'Maybe you'd like to come out with me next week?'

'The pictures again?' said Neela,

'If you like?'

'Or,' she said, 'we could go out for dinner.'

'Yes,' he said, hesitating.

'Of course,' she added, 'if you don't want to ...'

'Oh, but I do.' Doug leaned forward. 'I think you're the most attractive girl I've met in a long time.'

'Really?' She looked at him from under her eyelashes.

'Yes, really.'

'You're such a nice boy.' She patted his hand, and he tried to grasp hers, but she quickly withdrew it.

He didn't really want to be a nice boy—after all, at 23, he was old enough to marry, old enough to be a proper mechanic, to be on the way to owning his own business.

'I'll walk you home,' he offered.

'No,' she said quickly. 'You can walk me to the end of the street. You know how people gossip.'

At the end of the street, she turned to him and kissed him on the cheek. 'You really are nice, Doug, quite the nicest boy I've met for years.'

Doug walked home in a daze. Aunt Lizzie was sleeping in an armchair, Father was listening to the wireless, and Rona was tidying up in the kitchen.

'Have a good evening?' she asked.

'Yes.'

'Ooh, out with your pals, were you?'

Doug said nothing.

'Was it a good film?'

Doug nodded.

'Did she enjoy it?'

'I didn't say I'd been with a girl.'

'You didn't need to. You've got lipstick on your cheek.' Rona got up and yawned. 'I'm away to my bed. Some of us have to be up early.'

She turned towards the stairs.

Doug glared after her. Why couldn't his family mind their own business?

\*　　　\*　　　\*

Rona was serving a customer with potato scones when she heard a tap on the window and saw Callum making faces at her. She tried hard not to giggle, and did her best to concentrate on the customer.

'Will that be all?'

35

The woman hesitated, and looked at the cakes. 'I'm not sure. What are your cream cookies like?'

*Oh, do hurry up*, said Rona, though she said it to herself. At this rate Callum was going to give up and go away.

'I'll take two,' said the woman.

Oh, how slow she was! But at last she paid for the scones and cookies and stowed them in her basket. Rona saw she was inclined to talk. 'A fine breezy day,' she began.

'Thank you very much,' she said briskly 'I hope you enjoy the scones—freshly baked.'

She smiled at the woman, trying not to let her exasperation show, and finally the woman left the shop.

'I thought she'd never go,' said Rona as Callum pushed the door open.

He grinned at her. 'I've been waiting for you a good quarter-of-an-hour. Didn't you see me waving at you through the window?'

'You'll get me the sack,' she said solemnly.

'Well, anyway. Are you doing anything this evening? We could go to the pictures or maybe for a cup of coffee—there's that new coffee bar.'

'Oh, yes.' Rona had heard about the coffee bar. It was popular with the young folk of the town—there was a jukebox and they'd recently installed a television set.

\* \* \*

36

'Come on then.' He took her hand a little while later, and she wished she had been wearing elegant suede gloves instead of her old grey woollen gloves with a darn in the thumb. But it was still wintry and her old gloves and thick grey coat would have to do.

In the café, he fetched the cups of coffee from the counter along with a plate of biscuits.

'Not very exciting, I'm afraid.'

'They're fine.'

Rona glanced at the flickering black and white TV screen in the corner. 'I've never seen TV,' she said. 'It's marvellous.'

'One day,' he said, 'and it won't be all that long, everyone will have a television set in their living room.'

'Fat chance,' she said, laughing. 'You don't know my father and Aunt Lizzie. We've got an old wireless and that's about as far as they'll go.'

'Just like my folks. Not that there's much time to listen to the wireless—apart from the weather forecast. And sometimes Dad listens to *Farming Today*.'

'Aunt Lizzie doesn't even listen to the Scottish country dance programme,' said Rona gloomily.

'Your aunt—she's the one in the shop, isn't she?' Callum said, not liking to be inquisitive. 'Your mother—is she . . ?'

'She died when I was fifteen. Aunt Lizzie

came to look after us.'

Callum nodded, and remembering the grim figure behind the till, felt a wave of sympathy. What a dull home it must be, compared to his own. He thought of his own mother, placid and cheerful, always busy baking for the Rural or the Guild. She was good to the neighbours too—taking a bowl of soup or a plate of mince to anyone in trouble.

'And your mother?' Rona asked.

'She's all right,' said Callum.

'Have you always worked on the farm?' Rona stirred her coffee.

He nodded. 'Except for National Service. I'm . . .' he paused. 'I'm a bit fed up with it, I can tell you. I'd really like to go abroad, travel a bit.'

'You didn't travel when you were in the Army?'

He shook his head. 'No chance. Oh, it's not that I don't like farming, but I fancy trying my luck in Canada. I've a cousin who emigrated—he's got a shop now, near Montreal. Still, that's in the future. What about you?'

'I'd like to go to London—or even Edinburgh. I've never been to London. But there's not much chance of that.'

'So here we both are, stuck in Kirkton—for the moment, at least.' He grinned.

'Anyway, listen, do you like country dancing? There's a ceilidh on at that town hall next Saturday. What about it? With stovies at half time.'

'Sounds great.' Rona smiled. 'I'd really
enjoy that.'

* * *

'So,' said Nancy, the next day when she
caught up with Rona. 'What's he like then—a
dreamboat?'

'No,' Rona hesitated. 'I wouldn't say that,
but he's good fun.'

'Can't have everything,' said her friend. 'Did
I tell you about the man who came to repair
the typewriters?'

## CONFRONTING DOUG

'There was something else worrying Rona.
Once or twice she had seen Doug in the town
and he'd pretended not to see her. On two
separate occasions she had seen him helping
the same girl into the passenger seat.

She was very smart, thought Rona. I'd never
get away with all that make-up. Father would
have a fit if I wore all that eye makeup. And as
for Aunt Lizzie . . .

So where had he got the car? She had an
idea that as a mechanic at the garage, he
wasn't paid that much—certainly not enough
to buy a car.

He couldn't have . . . no, she pushed the thought away. Doug was honest as the day, he'd never think of *borrowing* a car.

But still, she was uneasy, and she decided that she must ask him, as tactfully as she could, who the car belonged to. It was all a matter of waiting for the right moment.

Meantime, Callum had dropped into the shop.

'OK to come to the ceilidh on Saturday?'

'I'd love to,' Rona paused as she carried a tray of sultana scones to the counter.

'Great. I'll see you outside the town hall at seven, if that suits you.'

'Fine.'

'I'd better be off. Your auntie's glowering at me.'

'Take no notice,' said Rona. 'See you Saturday.'

It was ages since she'd had a date. And Callum, well, he was good fun and it was time she had a little fun.

'What did that laddie want?'

Rona sighed. She might have known there was no escaping Aunt Lizzie's eagle eye.

'Nothing,' she said.

'Well,' said her aunt sternly. 'You'll have to tell him to stop coming into the shop for nothing. We're not a charity. And you gave him a free pie.'

'That was weeks ago.' Rona defended herself hotly.

40

'You tell him,' said Aunt Lizzie, 'either he comes in here and buys something like a proper customer or he stays away. I can see what he's after.'

'Oh, for goodness' sake!' Rona's temper flared up. 'Why shouldn't he come into the shop? Anyway, I'm going to the ceilidh with him on Saturday.'

'In my day,' said Aunt Lizzie, 'a young man knew his place and he'd ask her father's permission to take a young girl out.'

'This is nineteen fifty-two,' said Rona between gritted teeth. 'Not eighteen fifty-two.'

'I'll not have impertinence from you, miss.'

'What's all this about?' Angus appeared from the back of the shop. 'I can't have this argy-bargy in front of the customers.'

'There's no-one in the shop,' muttered Rona.

'I'm just telling your daughter,' said Aunt Lizzie, 'that she's not to encourage young men coming into the shop.'

Rona's face flushed. 'Why not? Anyway I'm going to the ceilidh with him on Saturday, whether you like it or not.'

'Well,' said Angus slowly. He was becoming rather tired of Aunt Lizzie, and her constant laying down of the law.

He looked at Rona and saw in her face in that moment how like her mother she was, and felt a sudden pang of loss. Oh, she was a bonnie one, this girl of his, and she was

41

growing up to look just like his Ruby.

It was Aunt Lizzie's dour expression that decided Angus. 'Oh, well, I can't see it'll do much harm going to the dancing, but you mind he brings you home and I don't want you out later than half-past ten.'

'Oh, thank you, Father!' Rona would have flung her arms round her father, except that they weren't the type to embrace.

'Well,' said Aunt Lizzie in a tight voice, 'of course, my opinion wasn't asked.'

'No,' said Angus, 'it wasn't, and now let's get on with the work. There's that order for the hotel, tomorrow, they want it by eleven o'clock.'

\*　　　\*　　　\*

Rona wished that she could have had a new dress for the dance, but knew that wasn't possible. She would have to make do with her pale blue wool dress, but she added a bow at the neckline and thought it looked right for the occasion.

You didn't want to look too dressed up for a ceilidh, but she brushed her hair until it shone and put on her best nylons, and made up carefully with her new Natural Rose lipstick, and a dash of Chypre, the scent that she'd bought with some of her Christmas present money. Her sandals were comfortable anyway and she hoped she'd be dancing all night.

42

Callum, when he met her, thought she looked a picture—that gorgeous hair, and her cheeks pink with excitement. 'You look grand,' he said awkwardly. He was not used to paying compliments to girls.

Clumsily, he steered her into the hall, and they paused almost deafened by the noise of the band—the band that was only the local band.

Everyone knew them. There was the postie on the accordion, and Johnnie Greig from the butcher's, thumping the drums as if his life depended on it. But to Rona, in her excitement, they seemed just as good as any dance band that you heard on the country dance programme on the wireless.

And the dance hall—well, Rona knew it was just the big room in the town hall, the hall they used for meetings, for flower shows and concerts. But tonight it was different, it was a special sort of feel about it.

'Take your partners for the Duke of Perth.'

Callum grabbed her by the hand and grinned at her. 'You know this one?'

She nodded, smiling. She'd enjoyed dancing at school and knew most of the dances. Callum was a good dancer and he whirled her round without any effort, and never once stepped on her toes.

'Come and meet some of my pals,' he said in a break between dances. They joined a noisy, laughing group—Rona knew some of them from years ago, the girl in the post office clinging to her boyfriend's arm, the fair-haired girl at reception in the dentist's surgery, one or two old school friends. Mostly they'd come with partners, but Rona was pleased she was with Callum.

Everyone seemed to like him and he was a better dancer than some of the others, she thought, after his friend, Tom, had tramped on her feet in an eightsome.

Sipping a lemonade, after a breathless whirl in the Gay Gordons, Rona thought she hadn't enjoyed an evening so much for a very long time.

'You look nice,' Callum told her shyly. Rona smiled to herself. She knew that Nancy's boyfriend, who worked in the same office, paid her extravagant compliments. Nancy had told her about some of the things he said. But Rona thought, I'd much rather have Callum's way of complimenting a girl. It sounded as if he meant it.

On the way home, he told her about the farm, about his older brother who would take over one day.

'What's it like, working for your father?' Rona asked.

He grimaced. 'Och, he's a hard man to please. Some days it's fine. Other days . . .' he broke off.

'I know what it's like,' said Rona. 'Working for your own father, and I've got my auntie in

44

the shop too. She can be so difficult. I wish she wouldn't keep picking on me, for every little thing.'

'She really scares me,' Callum confessed.

'That makes two of us,' said Rona and they both laughed.

'I think,' said Callum a little shyly, 'that folk come into the shop because of you. I mean, hoping you'll serve them.'

Rona blushed.

'I mean it,' he said. 'She puts people off, your auntie.'

'Oh, well,' said Rona. 'I'm stuck with the job, but I wish Father would let me do more— like decorating the window. And we could have a tearoom upstairs—plenty of bakers do. People would come in for their tea and coffee, and lots of people in the offices, for their dinner in the middle of the day.'

For a moment she had almost forgotten Callum and saw the tearoom of her imagination, just like McVitie's where she'd once been on a rare visit to Edinburgh.

There would be waitresses, well, maybe one waitress, trim in black with a white apron and cap, taking orders for toasted teacake and sultana scones.

Sometimes, she knew, tearooms had a piano tinkling in the background, and now and then the big stores would have a mannequin parade—a glamorous model moving among the tables, and stopping now and then to

45

answer a customer's query about the price, before gliding on with a gracious smile.

But no, she thought sadly, Father would never agree to having a tearoom.

'Penny for your thoughts,' said Callum.

She smiled. 'I was just thinking. Father would never agree to us having a tearoom— teas and coffees for the grand ladies who have time to go shopping, dinner for the people who are out at work and want a hot meal in the middle of the day.'

'So you and me,' said Callum, 'we're the same. We both work for our fathers, and we both want to do something different.'

'What do you want to do?' she asked.

'Go abroad for a bit,' he said. 'Maybe Canada. Ah, well,' he went on, 'I'm stuck here.'

They walked on in silence. 'I've got you home in time,' he said. 'I'm not wanting your father after me for keeping you out late.

'Listen,' he said, all in a rush, 'would you come out with me again? Maybe a bus run to Kirkcaldy or St Andrews when I have a half day? Or the pictures?'

'I'd like to.' She smiled up at him.

'I'll come into the shop,' he said. 'If I can beard your auntie in her den.' They both laughed at that.

'How are you getting back to the farm?' said Rona suddenly.

'I'll get a lift with one of my pals,' he said.

'Or I can walk. I have done before.'

'I really enjoyed the dancing.' Rona was suddenly shy.

For a moment she thought he was going to kiss her, but he just said, 'That's good, then. I did, too.' Then, 'I'll be seeing you,' and he was gone down the street with that long loping stride. She watched till he had turned the corner, then pushed open the gate.

Indoors there was no sign of her aunt—she must have gone to bed, and Angus turned in early, since he was always up by four to begin work.

Only Doug sat at the kitchen table, turning over the pages of a motoring magazine and listening idly to the wireless.

'Hello.' He didn't look up. 'Did you have a good time?'

'It was great.' Rona sank into a chair. 'You're not out tonight, then?' she asked.

'No.'

Doug was never one for much conversation, she thought. What did he and that girl talk about? But she'd heard him talking to one of his pals about cars, about the newest model, and problems with a starting handle, or a carburettor, and then he was voluble, even chatty.

She hesitated. 'I saw you with a girl.'

'Aye?'

'You and she were getting into a car—you were driving.' Rona thought, I am not handling

47

this right. 'The other evening.'

'Is that so?' Doug continued to scan the pages of the magazine, not looking at her.

Suddenly she burst out, 'Where did you get the car? You know you can't afford a car. And it was quite—' she paused, 'it was a posh car.'

He looked up and glowered at her—she had never seen her placid, easy-going brother look like this.

'And what's it to you?'

'I just wondered . . .' Rona ploughed on. She had got this far. 'I was worried. I mean, you can't afford a car and I thought, there's no-one we know has a car like that. Oh, Doug?' She hardly recognised her usually good-natured brother who glared at her across the table.

'It's nothing to do with you,' he said sharply. 'So why don't you mind your own business.' He flung the magazine aside and got up.

Rona gazed after him as he slammed out of the room. What was the matter? There was something badly wrong. And somehow the evening, with all its magic, was spoiled.

## REFLECTIONS FOR RONA

I'll soon be twenty-one and I haven't had any sort of life, thought Rona rebelliously. It should have been a good year, 1952, though it had begun on a sad note with the death of the

King in early February.

Aunt Lizzie had shaken her head sadly over the pictures in the paper of the three women all in black and heavily veiled—the Queen, now the Queen Mother, and Princess Elizabeth who had so suddenly become Queen, and her sister, Princess Margaret.

'Poor souls,' she said.

But then people talked about the future and the dawn of a new Elizabethan age. Now you could fly all over the world, there were all sorts of fascinating inventions—many people were buying or renting television sets, hoping to watch the coronation of the new Queen in June the next year.

All the same, for Rona, life seemed very flat and dull. The one bright spot was her friendship with Callum.

'Not a romance,' she told her friend, Nancy, hastily. 'We're just good friends.' But he made her laugh, and she enjoyed going dancing with him, or spending an evening at the pictures.

No, it was the feeling that life was going nowhere. She was stuck in Kirkton while other girls of her own age were working in Edinburgh or Glasgow, or even finding jobs abroad.

Father seemed to think that she was quite happy with the daily routine. She knew quite well that if she complained, he would look surprised and tell her she was lucky to have a good job.

And, of course, the main problem was Aunt Lizzie. There she was in the cash desk, 'And likely to be there for ever', thought Rona. She kept a watchful eye on everything that Rona did, and was quick to point out any mistakes, or take her to task for a job that wasn't properly done.

'Snappy old besom,' Rona often said under her breath and glared at Aunt Lizzie's back.

So the year wore on and every day seemed much like the one before.

It should have been a lovely summer's day. It looked so promising—yesterday had been fine and now the air was warm after the heat of the previous day. But it was a close, clammy sort of heat.

Rona, waking early, found nothing to look forward to. For one thing, she had a niggling toothache. She knew she should make an appointment with the dentist, but she had put it off. Maybe the pain will go away, she thought hopefully. But it didn't and by the time she reached the shop, she was feeling thoroughly miserable. It was going to be a very long day.

And of course Aunt Lizzie was in one of her most trying moods, finding fault with everything that Rona did. 'You've not swept the floor,' she said almost as soon as Rona had hung up her jacket.

'I'm just going to.' Rona gritted her teeth and then found that hurt.

There was no pleasing Aunt Lizzie today. She commented on Rona's overall. 'That needs a wash. You'd best give it to me and I'll see to it.'

'It was clean on yesterday.' Rona defended herself.

'Well, it doesn't look like it.' Aunt Lizzie sniffed and turned back to the till.

'I'm going to make a cup of tea.' Rona felt perhaps that might ease the pain a little. 'Can I make one for you?'

'No, thank you,' said Aunt Lizzie. 'I'm not one that needs to be always drinking tea. And you're just after your breakfast.'

This time Rona ignored her. Angus appeared from the back shop, wiping his forehead.

'It's going to be hot and sticky today. We'll maybe get thunder before the day's out.'

He nodded to them, and set out on his deliveries.

The morning dragged on. There were few customers and those few seemed to Rona to be trying. So many wanted to have a chat. She wasn't interested, she told herself, in this one's aches and pains, in another's new grandchild. And why should she be expected to care about someone's holiday plans, or the new caravan they had up on Deeside?

She tried to force a smile, without much success.

The shop was busy and there was hardly any

time for a break. Rona became more and more aware of her nagging tooth and Aunt Lizzie's constant complaints and criticisms seemed to hammer into her brain.

At last as it came to the dinner hour, Rona came to a decision. I don't have to stay here. Why should I? No-one appreciates me. She felt a great wave of self-pity, and all of a sudden she grabbed her handbag and rushed out of the door.

Behind her, Aunt Lizzie called, 'Where are you off to? It's not your dinner time.'

But Rona, hurrying down the High Street, didn't hear her. She had no idea where she was going—maybe to the promenade, maybe to the pier, or a café. She didn't care. As long as she could get away from Aunt Lizzie. And she told herself, 'That's it! I've had enough. I'm not going back—ever.'


## A CHANCE ENCOUNTER

Rona made her way along the High Street, aware that her blouse was clinging to her back and her hair felt damp on her forehead.

A breath of fresh air—that would help she decided as she took the turning that led to the promenade. She sank down on a seat overlooking the bay.

There was a pleasure steamer entering the

little harbour and one or two fishing boats. Normally she would have enjoyed watching the activity, but not today.

She sat miserably wondering what to do.

'I'm not going back—ever,' she thought.

It was then she heard the rumblings of thunder and now the first drops of rain began to fall. She got up hastily and began to hurry towards the town centre. By the time she reached the town hall and the shelter of its steps, her cardigan was soaked and her summer cotton dress clung damply to her body.

Breathless, she reached the shelter of the steps, and huddled there, watching the people scurrying along the pavement, nearly everyone taken unaware by the storm.

'Hey, what are you doing here?' It was a familiar voice.

'Callum. I could ask the same.'

'In the town for the market,' he said briefly. 'But you haven't got a waterproof or an umbrella. You're soaked.'

'I didn't bring a raincoat,' she said, shivering.

'Here,' he offered. 'You have my jacket. You'll want to get back.'

'No, thank you.'

'Oh, don't be stubborn, girl,' he said. 'Look at you, soaked through. Well, anyway, I'll come back to the shop with you.'

'I'm not going back,' she muttered.

'What do you mean?'

'I said, I'm not going back. I'm not going back to the shop ever again.'

He gave her a little shake. 'Don't be silly.'

'It's not silly. I'm determined. I've put up with Aunt Lizzie for ages, and I'm not standing for any more. She treats me like a child . . .' her voice tailed off.

'So?' said Callum.

'So that's it. I've finished with the shop. I'll get a job somewhere else. They can do without me.' She went on, 'I'm right, do you not agree?'

Callum said nothing. Then slowly, 'Well, it's your decision.'

'You think I'm in the wrong, then?' Rona flared up.

'I didn't say that. I said it's up to you.'

'But surely,' she persisted, 'you can see that I'm just treated like a skivvy.'

'Well . . .' said Callum thoughtfully.

Rona was angry by now. 'You're siding with them. You don't think I'm within my rights to walk out, do you?'

'No,' he said. 'I don't. You do a good job there, and your father relies on you. I think you're being hasty and you'll be sorry later on.'

'Oh, I'll be sorry, will I?' Rona glared at him.

'Come on, Rona,' he said. 'This isn't like you. Usually you're good-tempered. Is there something else the matter, not just Aunt

54

Lizzie?'

She stepped back, bumping into a man who was coming out of the town hall. 'Watch it, miss,' he said.

'So what's wrong?' Callum asked in a gentle tone.

Rona suddenly burst into tears. 'I'm miserable. I've got toothache, and I'm wet and cold and I hate the job.'

'Oh, you poor thing.' Callum put his arms round her, and they both ignored the people who were going in and out of the town hall, and glancing at the couple who were standing there, oblivious.

'You poor wee soul,' Callum said as he held her close.

Rona raised her head. 'I've made your shirt all damp,' she sniffed.

'Never mind that. Here, I insist that you can have my jacket, and I'll walk back with you to the shop.' He draped his jacket over her shoulders. 'Come on, the rain isn't as heavy now.'

'But . . .' she began to protest.

'Look,' he said. 'This is what I think you should do. You go back to work, tell your father and Aunt Lizzie you've got toothache and go straight along to the dentist and tell them it's an emergency. If it's Mr Anderson— he's your dentist, isn't he? He'll see you right away. And don't think any more for the moment about leaving the job. Wait till you're

55

a bit calmer, and then decide.'

Rona sniffed again. 'All right.' She managed a faint smile. 'If I hadn't met you, I'd probably have been at the station catching the next train to Edinburgh or Dundee or anywhere.'

'Then it's a good thing we met,' he said, smiling at her. 'Come on, let's hurry.'

When they reached the shop, Rona handed back his jacket. By now the rain had almost stopped.

'Will you come in?' she said.

'No thanks, I'd better get back to work. And besides, you know I'm scared of your aunt.' He grinned. 'I'll be seeing you.' He gave her a quick hug and disappeared.

Rona pushed open the door, and drew a deep breath. Aunt Lizzie was sure to be angry with her.

Yet Aunt Lizzie hardly looked up from the invoices she was checking. 'Oh, there you are. A bit late, aren't you? Where did you get to? Did you get caught in the rain?' she said a little absently.

'Oh, I just popped out for my lunch break,' said Rona. 'I'm back again.'


## TROUBLE FOR DOUG

'Well, here's a pretty kettle of fish!' Aunt Lizzie laid down the letter she had been reading.

'What's the matter?' Rona was just about to leave for work.

'It's that sister-in-law of mine.'

'Maisie?'

'Her. In Glencraig,' said Aunt Lizzie in a tone of voice which seemed to indicate that Maisie had no business in Glencraig or anywhere else. 'Typical!'

Rona swallowed a last piece of toast.

'What's she done? Only gone into hospital.'

Rona paused, 'Oh, I'm sorry.' She had met Maisie only once, and found her a gentle soul, no match for Aunt Lizzie's powerful personality.

'What's wrong with her?'

'It's her insides,' said Lizzie delicately. There were some things not to be spoken of in front of a girl Rona's age.

'Anyway,' she went on, 'she's coming out of hospital Friday and wants me to go up to help out in the house.'

Rona remembered the house, a low rambling cottage on the outskirts of Glencraig.

'And will you?'

'Go up there? There's no-one else to cope, I suppose I'll have to. She's a fushionless one,' she dismissed her sister-in-law. 'But I was fond of George.'

Rona had heard often about George, Lizzie's brother, and the bright one of the family. Dux at the school, training to be a lawyer, and then the War came. He was badly injured at Dunkirk and never recovered his health.

He had slipped out of life, quietly, leaving his widow, Maisie, alone with no family—except for Lizzie. 'She's feckless,' said Aunt Lizzie bracingly, 'depended on him for everything.'

'So will you go?' A wild hope seized Rona. She was sorry for Maisie, of course she was, but might Aunt Lizzie actually hurry to take charge of the house in Glencraig?

Might she leave Father and Doug and Rona to shift for themselves? It was a wild, improbable hope.

This thought had clearly occurred to Aunt Lizzie. 'I'll have to go, of course,' she said, 'but what's going to happen here while I'm away?'

'We'll manage.' Rona tried to sound as if she were going to cope bravely 'We'll do our best.'

After all, she was nearly 21 now. And look at the responsibilities some carried—some only a few years older. She thought of the new young Queen, only 26, and soon to be crowned.

'Aye,' said Aunt Lizzie doubtfully. 'Aye, well . . .' Already her thoughts were some distance away 'I could get the bus to Dunfermline, then the train—there's one goes through Kinross and Glenfarg to Perth. If I got off at Glenfarg . . . I'll write to her today—say I'll be up on

58

Friday.'

'I'd better be off,' said Rona hurriedly. 'I'll tell Father.'

She tried not to skip as she went down the path. All on their own without Aunt Lizzie disapproving of everything. Then she slowed down. Poor Maisie. It was hard on her, but all the same every cloud has a silver lining, she told herself.

In the past few weeks, Rona had decided not to let herself be upset by Aunt Lizzie.

She would not fly off the handle again, but would try to be calm and cheerful and ignore her aunt's sarcastic remarks—after all, she thought, Aunt Lizzie wasn't going to change, so I might as well accept her ways.

Callum had been right. There was no point in walking out in a temper. Much better to wait until she had a definite plan for the future.

For Rona had not given up the idea of becoming a model. She studied the fashion magazines and in the privacy of her bedroom practised walking with a copy of *Familiar Quotations*—a heavy tome, balanced on her head.

And she hugged to herself, her big idea. The Coronation of Queen Elizabeth the Second was to be in June. A special window? Maybe she should persuade Father? After all, it would bring more business into the shop.

\*　　　\*　　　\*

Angus was taking a tray of new baked rolls from the oven.

'I'll be off on the deliveries then,' he said. 'Seeing you're here. Where's your aunt?'

Rona explained.

'You can tell me later,' he said. 'Folk will be wanting their rolls for their breakfast.'

He looked at her doubtfully. 'You'll have to manage the till today—just until we get someone else. Ah, well, we'll have to cope. See and keep the shop tidy, and don't drop anything.'

And with that, he was off on the first delivery to the big hotel overlooking the sea.

The day was busy as usual. Rona was kept hard at work, explaining that her aunt was leaving for Glencraig the next day. 'I'll not be in the shop today,' Aunt Lizzie had announced. 'You'll have to shift without me. This place is like a midden.' She had glanced round at the kitchen.

To Rona, it seemed immaculate, the wooden draining board scrubbed white, pots and pans neatly arranged on a shelf, taps polished.

When Angus returned from his rounds, he noticed approvingly that Rona had swept the floor of the shop and tidied the shelves.

'Aye,' he said, 'not bad. Now you think you can manage the till, for a day or so, till I see about things. We'll need to get someone in

60

to help. I'll go along to the Labour Exchange if I've time. Or I could put an advert in the paper.'

'No bother,' said Rona airily. 'Father, can I do a window for the Coronation?'

'Don't bother me just now, there's a good girl,' said Angus.

'Later,' said Rona to herself, 'I'll ask again!'

Back home, Aunt Lizzie had already packed her suitcase, and now she was scouring the kitchen. She'd drawn up a list of meals for the next few days.

'You can have mince tomorrow,' she told Rona. 'And tell the butcher I always have the best quality mince. There's plenty of potatoes and carrots. And I've made a blancmange for your pudding. Oh, and there's enough soup to do you two or three days!' She sighed. 'How you're going to manage, I've no idea.'

'Don't you fret yourself,' said Angus. 'We'll shift fine. Rona here's a good little housewife already.'

Aunt Lizzie sniffed. 'Well, she'll have to learn.'

She left the next day with a large leather suitcase and a grim expression. Rona couldn't help feeling a little sorry for Maisie—she was sure there would not be much sympathy from Aunt Lizzie.

But as soon as she had gone the air somehow seemed lighter. Aunt Lizzie had left stew to be heated up. 'There's just the potatoes to peel,' she had told Rona. 'You can manage that all right, can't you?'

*    *    *

Callum called in at the shop.

'I'm just in the town to collect an order at the ironmonger's,' he said. 'What about the pictures or the dancing, maybe tomorrow night?'

'Oh, Callum,' she said, disappointed, 'I can't—not this week.' She explained about Aunt Lizzie's departure. 'And I've got to make the dinner for Father and Doug.'

'Maybe Saturday, just a walk along the front? Pity to waste these fine evenings.'

'All right. I'm sure I can manage.'

'Great. I'll wait for you outside your house—say six o'clock.'

Rona's spirits lifted. With Aunt Lizzie away there would be more freedom. She would be able to go out with Callum, she'd have a free hand with the meals, and at the shop, she would be in charge—well, not quite, but at least she would be supervising the new girl when they found someone. Rona knew exactly the sort of person she wanted.

Someone who never said a word, but was obliging and what's more, would do as Rona told her.

*    *    *

Later that evening, Angus lit his pipe and settled back in his armchair with the evening paper.

'Grand dinner.'

'Aunt Lizzie left it,' said Rona. 'It's me cooking from now on.'

His eyes twinkled as he looked at her over his glasses. 'Well, we'll need to stock up on the indigestion tablets, won't we?'

'Oh, you . . .' she said, pretending to be offended.

'By the way,' said Angus, 'where's your brother? He's not been in for his meal.'

'I don't know.' Rona and Doug had barely spoken since their row over the car.'

'He'll be out somewhere.'

But she was worried—what had happened to Doug?

It was much later, when Angus had gone to bed, that Doug stumbled through the door.

'Where have you been?' Rona spoke sharply, trying not to show how anxious she was. 'Your dinner's in the oven, but it'll be dried up by now.'

'I don't want any dinner.'

'Doug! What's happened? What's the matter?'

'Oh, nothing.' He tried to sound off-hand.

'Don't be stupid. Tell me.'

'Keep your voice down. You'll waken Father.'

'What has happened?' said Rona in a loud whisper.

'Oh, well, if you must know, the car crashed into a ditch.'

'Oh, no!'

'Oh, yes,' he said, mocking her.

'But I thought you were a good driver.'

'I wasn't driving. Neela was. Or rather I was teaching her to drive.'

'And?' Rona was nearly speechless. 'Whose car was it? Oh, Doug, you didn't borrow it, you didn't—steal it?'

'What do you take me for?' His voice rose again. 'I'm not a thief.'

'Then where did you get it?'

'It was Neela's brother's car. He's away abroad for a couple of months. He said I could drive it—if I was careful. But she insisted she wanted to learn to drive. And now, well it's in a ditch up the Bridge Road. I wish,' he added bitterly, 'I had never set eyes on that stupid woman.'

## ANGUS DESPAIRS

'You're a fool, Doug.'Angus was really angry. It took a lot to rile him for he was generally a placid man. 'What on earth possessed you to take up with a girl like that?'

He sighed and rubbed his brow. 'As if there

weren't enough nice lassies around.'

There had been no keeping from Angus the whole business of the car, and it came out too, that he knew of Neela and her reputation in the town as something of a party girl. 'She's been nothing but trouble, that girl,' he went on rubbing salt into the wound. 'And you'll have to pay for any repairs—and face up to her brother.'

It was then he felt he had said plenty. Doug, sitting at the kitchen table, looked miserable enough, but a moment later Angus couldn't resist adding, 'If your mother had lived to see the day . . . and it's maybe just as well your aunt Lizzie's not here.'

Doug roused himself to say, 'The garage got the car out of the ditch and it's not badly damaged. Just a headlamp dented.'

'Aye well,' said Angus.

'And she, Neela, said she'll pay for the damage,' Doug went on.

'Aye, well. You've learned your lesson and you'll stay away from her in future. She's nothing but trouble, and you're not the first one to find out either apparently.'

'I'm away out.' Doug got up and Rona followed him out of the door.

She hadn't the heart to say, 'You might at least help with the dishes.'

She had never seen Doug, her cheerful, good-natured brother, look so woebegone.

Doug, who could always make her laugh

with his Charlie Chaplin imitations, or stories of the other lads at the garage—he looked as if his world had fallen apart.

Rona realised it was not so much the damage to the car that was upsetting him. That could be fixed, but the damage to his pride, the knowledge that Neela didn't care a bit for him, that she was only out for a good time—that was what hurt.

'There're other girls,' she said a little timidly.

'I never want to see her again. Her brother blamed me, for letting her drive the car, and you'd think it was my fault she steered into a ditch. She's got no sense at all,' he added morosely.

'Oh, Doug, forget it. No-one was hurt.' Rona tried to cheer him.

'That's right. Well, it's a good thing Aunt Lizzie is away. I'd never have heard the end of it.' He gave a weak attempt at a grin. 'I'm away down to the harbour—there's some of the boats coming in.'

Rona waved and turned back into the house. Yes, she thought, Aunt Lizzie's absence was a blessing in disguise, even if it did mean extra work.

Washing, ironing, cooking—though Father was good and cleaned out the grate before he left for the shop, and made sure there was enough kindling, and the meals, well, they weren't bad at all. Rona had glowed with pride when Angus had commented, 'Your mince is just as good as your auntie's.'

There had only been a brief postcard from Aunt Lizzie to say Maisie was still in hospital and wouldn't be home for another week. 'We'll need to get someone to help in the shop,' said Angus thoughtfully. 'Maybe a lassie to do some of the cleaning and serve, if you can manage the till,' he told Rona who was rather proud of her position .

*　　　*　　　*

Rona was wrapping up a customer's brown loaf the next day when she heard an apologetic cough.

'Oh, good morning, Mr Grey. A fine morning,' said Rona politely.

The lawyer nodded pleasantly. 'And good morning to you, Miss Maclaren,' he returned.

Rona liked Mr Grey, the lawyer who rented the floor above the bakery. He was middle-aged, with sparse greying hair and a neat moustache and she knew that day in, day out, he always ordered a small pan loaf.

'The usual, Mr Grey?'

'Thank you, yes, Miss Maclaren.'

Rona sometimes wondered what his wife was like. Was she as orderly, or would she perhaps have sometimes liked to throw caution to the wind and order a large brown wholemeal?

She liked Miss Mackie, Mr Grey's secretary too—invariably trim and neatly dressed in a heather tweed suit and a grey jumper hand knitted in three-ply, her hair permed in small grey curls.

It seemed as if Miss Mackie had been there as long as Rona could recall—she remembered coming into the shop as a small girl and meeting the gentle-voiced woman, who'd seemed middle-aged even then.

Miss Mackie lived with an elderly mother, she knew that. Once or twice a week Miss Mackie would come down from the office upstairs and buy bread and scones. 'Oh, and I'll take four pancakes, please—they're Mother's favourite.'

Every Christmas, Angus would send upstairs two boxes of shortbread, one for Mr Grey and one for Miss Mackie, and back downstairs would come a bottle of whisky for Angus—though he drank little and it would probably last a year or more, he appreciated the gesture.

Last Christmas, too, there had been a bottle of Yardley's Lavender Water for Aunt Lizzie and a box of handkerchiefs for Rona—chosen, she suspected, by Miss Mackie.

'Will that be all?' asked Rona politely as she wrapped the loaf.

'Thank you.' He looked rather preoccupied this morning, she thought. Could there be something wrong?

He turned and went upstairs again by

the outside stair that led to the firm's rented offices.

Angus, coming into the shop, nodded to him.

'I'm away on the rounds, Rona,' he said. 'I'll need to send you along with the advert.'

He sighed. 'It makes extra work, your aunt Lizzie away, we could do with a message girl. Still, we'll just have to manage as best we can.'

He didn't add, 'with you,' though Rona could see the thought crossing his mind.

'I'm not that bad,' she told herself rebelliously. 'I haven't made any mistakes for a long time. If he'd only let me do a bit more.'

'Here you are,' he handed her the slip of paper.

'I don't know why we put the advert into *The Advertiser*,' Rona muttered. 'It never alters from week to week. Just *Maclaren's Baker's, High Street* and a line above. *Rhubarb tarts, strawberry tarts, black bun* . . . whatever the season. Father's got no idea.'

She took the paper as her father hurried out of the shop. 'Rhubarb tarts,' she read. 'How's that for an advert? Customers know we have rhubarb tarts. We have rhubarb tarts every year, and we'll have them till the end of time.'

She waited till her father had gone out of the shop and it was quiet and she picked up a pencil. After a moment's thought she scrawled on the paper and looked at it approvingly.

Then she collected her coat, turned the sign

to *Closed 1 till 2*, and made her way along the street to the offices of the local newspaper.

'Right you are,' said the girl in the advertising department. She stopped filing her nails and took the piece of paper. 'Same as usual,' she said in a bored voice, 'and invoice at the end of the month.'

'Thank you' As Rona set off along the street again she began to have misgivings. What if Father was cross with her? Well, she reasoned, it was worth a try. If it brought in new business, he would be only too pleased.

He kept saying that they had to do their best for the customers. Rona grimaced. That didn't mean he would allow her a free hand with the window—and those tins of shortbread had been there for ages, she thought, exasperated.

It wasn't till the local paper appeared at the end of the week that Angus saw what Rona had done. He was skimming through the pages, past accounts of retirements, town council business, sheep dog trials, that his eye was caught by Maclaren's advertisement down the page in the same place as usual. But as he read it, his face grew redder and he flung down the paper. 'What's this?'

'Oh, dear.' Rona in the front shop, knew what was corning. 'Yes, Father?' she said trying to look unconcerned.

Hardly able to speak, he pointed at the advert. 'This is your doing,' he said. 'Am I right?'

'Well . . .' Rona hesitated. 'I thought it might make it a little more interesting.'

'Rhubarb tarts—the best you'll find in Kirkton from Maclaren's, the best baker in Kirkton! Fit for a Queen!'

'I just thought,' said Rona in a small voice. She had been rather proud of that line, *Fit for a Queen*. Of course, it was unlikely that the new young Queen, Elizabeth the Second, would be passing through a small town in Fife and would stop to buy one of Maclaren's rhubarb tarts, but you never knew. And they were very good.

'And this line, *the best baker in Kirkton*.' Angus thumped the paper. 'We'll be in trouble—that's for sure.'

Trouble arrived a day later when Henry Duncan, owner of Keith's, the rival bakery in the Square, appeared in the shop.

'Is your father in?'

'I'll fetch him.' Rona knew very well what Mr Duncan wanted. Normally a cheerful, good-natured man today he scowled at her and she hurried into the back shop.

'Well, Angus, what's this about?' Henry Duncan laid the paper on the counter. 'I'm surprised at you putting out an advert like this.'

For once Angus had nothing to say.

'I take it you don't know much about the law, the law of libel that is, for all you've a lawyer upstairs from your shop.'

71

Angus started to apologise.

'The damage is done,' said Henry Duncan. 'It seems to me you've taken leave of your senses.'

Rona could bear it no longer. She took off her overall and stepped out from the back shop.

'It was me, Mr Duncan,' she said, her voice quavering.

'You?'

'Father told me to take the advert along to *The Advertiser*'s office,' she said, 'and I thought . . .' she gulped, 'I thought I'd make it a bit more interesting.'

'Interesting!' Henry Duncan roared. 'And you thought you'd ruin my business on the way?'

'I'm sorry,' said Rona humbly. 'I didn't think.'

'Obviously not,' said Henry Duncan, and then because he was a fair man and had a sense of humour, he gave a roar of laughter.

'You thought you'd do a bit of good publicity,' he said, chuckling. 'Well, you're an enterprising young lady, that's for sure. Maybe you should come and work for me.'

Rona sighed with relief. 'I'm truly sorry,' she said again.

'We'll say no more about it,' said Henry. 'Least said, soonest mended, eh, Angus?'

'That's fair of you in the circumstances,' said Angus.

72

'Ah, well, let's hope it does no harm to my business, but local folk know a good rhubarb tart when they taste one.'

Still chuckling, he closed the door behind him.

'Let this be a lesson to you.' Angus was not going to let Rona off lightly 'Henry was fair about it, I'll give him that.'

He paused. 'And another thing, I've been thinking. Now that your auntie's away, we need an extra assistant for the shop. I'd better draft the ad myself,' he said.

The door bell tinkled as an elderly woman appeared at the door of the shop. 'Have you any of these rhubarb tarts—the ones that were in *The Advertiser*?'

'Of course.'

'*Fit for a Queen*, it said.'

'They're—' Rona paused, not wanting to get into trouble again. 'They're very good.'

'I'll take one.' The woman paused. 'I cut out all the pictures of the Queen—her and Prince Philip, and the Queen Mother too.'

'Do you?'

'She's a fine young woman and she'll make a grand Queen. My, I'd like to be at the Coronation come June, but we'll maybe see it on the television. And four of your soda scones, as well,' she added, changing tack.

'Enjoy the rhubarb tart,' said Rona. If the ad was bringing in business, it hadn't hurt the baker's, she thought.

'I've come for one of your rhubarb tarts,' said the next customer. 'Are they as good as it said in the paper?'

'Every bit as good,' said Rona loyally.

At the end of the morning she told Angus, 'We're sold out of rhubarb tarts.'

She would have liked to put one in the window, maybe with a ticket, *As advertised in the Kirkton Advertiser*, but felt that might be going too far.

'It's the power of the Press,' she said to Angus. 'They're all wanting these rhubarb tarts.'

'Sold out, eh?' he said. 'And to think I just fancied one for our tea.'

He shook his head at her and Rona knew she was forgiven.


## HELP FOR RONA

'A school-leaver would do us fine,' said Angus. 'A bright lad, or a girl, willing to learn.' He paused his pencil over the sheet of paper. 'No, a girl's better. A lad would be wanting to learn to drive the van.'

He wrote carefully, *Female shop assistant wanted* and added, *Apply to Maclaren's, High Street*

'There, we'll see what that brings in.'

The first applicant was clearly unsuitable,

74

though Rona rather liked her. She was tall with a shock of red hair. She was wearing pale blue trousers which Rona recognised as the latest fashion, *pedal pushers*, she said to herself, a red and white striped top and large sunglasses, though it was a cool day with grey skies that threatened rain.

'I've come for the job.'

'This way,' said Rona, wondering with a grin what Angus would make of this apparition.

The interview didn't last long. The girl emerged from the back premises, she shrugged her shoulders and threw a pitying glance at Rona. 'Do you work here all the time?'

'Yes.' said Rona defensively 'My father's the owner of the business.' She thought 'the business' sounded grander than just 'the shop'.

'Is he now?' The girl shook her head slowly. 'My, my. Poor you. I've other interviews so I'd best get along. Ta, ta.' She slammed the door behind her.

Rona was a little sorry that this was not to be the new assistant.

'Wouldn't do at all,' said Angus. 'There's bound to be other applicants.'

But there were not many, and none of them suitable, though Rona rather liked one girl who had a loud cheery laugh. She could see that they might have had a lot of fun together, but Angus shook his head. 'Wouldn't do at all, that one,' he said firmly. 'That laugh, it would drive me demented in a day.'

The last applicant was a small girl with mousy hair and pale, sharp features. Her hair was cut short and she wore a grey knitted jumper and a pleated skirt, shabby, but clean.

'I've come about the advertisement that was in the paper,' she said in a small voice.

'You'd better come through.'

She was very slight, thought Rona, would this one be strong enough for the job?

'I've got a reference. The girl produced from her basket a much folded piece of paper and thrust it towards Rona.

'It's my father that's interviewing,' said Rona, a little regretfully. 'You'll have to see him.'

'Right then,' said Angus appearing from the back shop. 'Now miss, what's your name?'

'I'm Jean Ross,' said the girl, 'but they call me Jeannie.' The words came out in a little squeak.

Angus scanned the piece of paper she held out to him which told him that Jean Ross had been a conscientious and hardworking pupil, and neat and tidy in her work.

He explained the demands of the job. 'It's hard work.'

'I'm not afraid of hard work,' she said with a little spurt of spirit.

'And early rising,' he added. 'The shop's open at eight for people wanting breakfast rolls.'

'I'm always up early,' she said a little

defiantly.

'Right you are.' There was not much left to say, except for discussion of wages and her insurance stamp and time off. 'A half day a week, and a week's holiday in the summer.'

She was not ideal. He would have liked a big, strong girl capable of handling the large trays of loaves and rolls, but he was anxious to fill the post.

'She'll have to do,' he said to Rona as he ushered the girl out of the shop.

'You start on Monday, Jeannie. Mind, eight sharp.'

Rona was a little disappointed. She would have liked someone a bit brighter, someone you could share a joke with. And what about Aunt Lizzie when she came back again?

Poor Jeannie, she thought. If she was in awe of Father, she would be absolutely terrified of Aunt Lizzie.

But Maclaren's were taking on staff and this new girl would be under Rona's supervision.

'Fancy me with a junior assistant,' thought Rona, and liked the idea.


AN UNFORTUNATE OCCURRENCE

The new assistant, Jeannie, proved to be a willing worker—she scurried backwards and forwards, and to Rona's surprise, was

77

much stronger than she looked, lifting trays without much effort and sweeping the floor energetically.

Rona rather enjoyed being in charge of her, and clearly Jeannie looked up to Rona and was willing to do whatever Rona asked.

Sometimes Rona tried to draw her out, but there was no talk of home or boyfriends or outings. Once Rona had suggested an evening at the pictures, but Jeannie shook her head. 'I've things to do at home,' so Rona gave up. 'If she doesn't want to, that's it.'

But she liked the quiet little girl, always in her spotless white pinafore, and having Jeannie as an extra hand certainly made things easier in the shop.

It was a good thing Aunt Lizzie was still away, Rona smiled to herself. She could just imagine how Jeannie would be terrified of Aunt Lizzie. Even Callum's scared of her, thought Rona.

She wondered for a moment how Aunt Lizzie was getting on, and whether she and Maisie were still on speaking terms. There had been a postcard or two, but her aunt would never think of phoning. She regarded the phone as a needless extravagance.

\*     \*     \*

It was perhaps a few weeks later that the trouble began. Rona had risen early. Now that

78

the days were lighter, she liked to hear the dawn chorus and usually lay awake for a little while listening, but she had to be at the shop by eight, and there was no time for dreaming.

It was going to be a bright day, she thought as she dressed, glancing out of the window at the garden, springing into life now. The daffodils against the wall were a cheerful patch of colour and soon the wallflower and dwarf tulips under the window would be out and every day would be warmer.

Angus was busy making up the orders when she arrived and she sniffed, enjoying as she always did, the smell of freshly baked rolls.

'We're needing some more paper bags,' he said a little later. 'Away you go along to Grant's and get say, four dozen. Get a receipt, remember and take the money out of the petty cash.'

Rona opened the cash box that was kept on a ledge behind the counter, and locked away every night. 'There's nothing in the box, Father,' she said.

'Nonsense. There must be. There's two or three pounds there. I put the money in myself yesterday. Did you lock it away last night?'

Rona tried to remember. She'd been hurrying to get away to meet Callum as they were going to the pictures and she'd promised to be at the Regal on time so they wouldn't miss the big picture.

'I . . . I can't remember.'

'You mean you didn't.' Angus stared at the empty box.

'I've the petty cash records here,' Rona said. She'd been careful about checking the petty cash, as instructed by Aunt Lizzie. 'And all the receipts, but there's been nothing paid out for the last few weeks, not since . . .' she checked the slips, 'not since I bought tea and sugar, and that was a week or two back.'

'And I've topped up the tin every week,' said Angus, puzzled. 'A couple of pounds at a time, in shillings and florins mostly, the odd half crown. There's a note in the box.'

'But . . .' he shook the box, 'there's nothing left.' He looked serious. 'It would seem to me that money's going missing from the petty cash. As if I hadn't enough to think about. And where's the girl?'

A few moments later, the door burst open and Jeannie hurried in. 'I'm that sorry,' she said. 'I couldn't get away from home on time.'

'You should have been here at eight,' said Angus coldly. 'That's the terms of your employment. If you're going to keep coming in late . . .'

'I'm sorry,' she apologised, flushing. 'It'll not happen again.'

'Well, you'd better get your apron on and get down to work,' he said. 'Rona, you and I will have to sort out this business of the money. I don't like to think . . . .' he paused. 'Ah well.'

He glanced at Jeannie. Surely not . . .

They decided that he should put an extra couple of pounds in the box and mark the notes. 'That way,' he said, 'if anyone's coming in to the shop and knows where the box is, we'd be certain to catch them red handed.' He shook his head. 'I don't like it. I've never had this kind of thing before, never in all the years.' His voice tailed off.

It was perhaps a couple of weeks later that Angus took the box to lock it away for the night. That was odd, he thought. It felt light, though he'd put in two or three pounds and some small change only that morning.

But now the box was empty.

He was at work next thy early as usual, and Jeannie, who had as she promised turned up on time every day, arrived just after him.

The morning was busy, there were orders to get out for two boarding houses in the town, and a special delivery of teacakes and sultana and cherry slab cake to the town hall for an afternoon function.

So it was not until the shop was quiet later on, that Jeannie approached him hesitantly.

'I was wondering, Mr Maclaren, could I take my dinner-break early? I'm wanting to get to the shops before one.'

'Aye, that'll be all right,' he said a little absently. And then he thought. 'Jeannie, I'm not saying anything, but did you open the petty cash box yesterday?'

81

Rona, tidying the shelves, turned sharply. Surely Father wasn't accusing Jeannie?

Jeannie's face flushed. 'Me? Me, Mr Maclaren? What would I be wanting with the petty cash box?'

'You were the only one here,' he returned. 'Mind you, I'm not saying anything.'

He hesitated a moment. 'I wouldn't like to suspect anyone, so you'll not mind if I ask you to open your purse.'

Jeannie went to her coat hanging in the back shop and produced a shabby leather purse.

'You'll open it, please. You understand?' Angus was a fair man. 'You were the only one here, so I have to be certain. Just a precaution.'

Very slowly she opened the purse and laid out the heap of sixpences, a few shillings and two ten-shilling notes.

Angus picked up the notes and held them out to her. 'They're marked,' he said. 'These were the ones I marked.'

Jeannie stared at him, horrified. Then she burst into tears. 'I never meant to,' she sobbed. 'I needed the money. I was going to put it back, honest.'

'Honest?' Angus's voice rose. 'You don't know the meaning of the word. And how long has this been going on?'

'It was just a little at first—maybe a shilling or two.' She spoke so quietly, that Rona,

82

standing behind the counter, could hardly hear her.

Angus looked at her coldly. 'I can't have anyone working here that I can't trust,' he said. 'Miss Maclaren here will give you your money till the end of the week and you can go now. Fetch your coat and get out.'

'Father!' said Rona.

'Be quiet, Rona, this is nothing to do with you.'

'But you're being unfair. It could have been anyone. It could have been me.'

'But it wasn't, was it, Rona?' He glared at her.

'No, of course not,' she said hotly.

'Well, there's only one thief here, and it's been proved. Go on, girl, get your wages from Miss Maclaren and you can be off.'

Jeannie was silent. She didn't look at Rona and in a few minutes she was gone, closing the door quietly behind her.

'Well,' said Angus heavily, 'we'd best get back to work. I'm just thankful the shop was empty.'

There was something very strange about the whole situation, thought Rona. She knew there was no use talking to Father, but she was determined to get to the bottom of it.

# A LESSON OF LIFE

It was perhaps a fortnight later, a pleasant late spring evening with a slight breeze, when Callum and Rona met up.

'There's nothing much on at the pictures,' he said. 'Fancy a walk? We could go down by the harbour and along the sands.'

'Fine.'

'And maybe stop for an ice-cream if the café's still open.'

'I'd like that.'

They set off down the road that led to the harbour. Rona had often wondered about these little houses—all in a row, they must be cramped inside and no front garden like the ones they'd just passed which were bright with late tulips and wallflowers.

As they approached one of the houses, Rona thought that it looked just like all the rest, except there was a figure bent double who seemed to be whitening the step. The woman—no, it was a girl—looked up and seeing Rona, looked away again quickly and bent down to her work.

'Callum,' said Rona, 'would you mind walking on? I'll catch up with you in a minute. There's . . . someone I know, I want to speak to.'

'Right you are.' Callum was good-natured as

84

always. 'I'll wait for you on the pier.'

Rona watched him as he walked away, then turned to the girl who had ignored her.

'Jeannie?'

Jeannie looked up, the brush in her hand. 'Did you want something?' she said in a flat sort of tone.

'Not really. We were just passing. I, er, I didn't know you lived here.'

'Well, we do.' Jeannie was not prepared to say more. 'A fine evening,' she blurted out, looking awkward.

'You're busy.' Rona hesitated.

'Aye. Did you want something?' Jeannie repeated.

'No, I wasn't spying or anything,' said Rona hastily.

Jeannie looked up and down the narrow street. 'Do you want to come in? Folk are gossips round here.'

'Just for a moment. Callum and I are out for a walk.'

She followed Jeannie into the little house. There was a narrow passageway and off it a small living room with a table, a couple of dining chairs and an easy chair.

Beyond, Rona could see a scullery. At the dining room table sat a boy about twelve years old, a jotter and book spread out in front of him.

'I'm sorry about the smell of fish,' Jeannie apologised. 'There's a man at the harbour

85

gives me the odd whiting.' She sniffed. 'We had it for our tea.'

She turned to the boy. 'Say hello to Miss Maclaren, Tommy,' she said sharply. 'And then you take your books to the bedroom.' The boy muttered a shy, 'Hello,' and disappeared.

'I didn't know you had a brother,' said Rona.

'Two,' said Jeannie briefly. 'The other one's George. He's in his bed. He's not that well.' A shadow crossed her face.

Rona hesitated then said all in a rush, 'I'm sorry about what happened.'

'Fair enough,' said Jeannie, and Rona, surprised, thought how much more confident she seemed in her own home. 'I was caught stealing and any boss would have sacked me.'

'But,' Rona was puzzled. 'Why?'

'I needed the money. Tommy needs new boots for the school and I want him to have a blazer. How do you think I could afford these things? And George needs to be kept warm so there's money needed for coal.'

Rona was silent for a moment, then she said, ' But do you pay for all this? I mean—'

She knew that Jeannie hadn't earned a great deal at the baker's.

'I work in the evenings, cleaning offices and sometimes up at the caravans,' said the girl. 'He's clever, Tommy,' said Jeannie, fiercely proud, 'and he's going to have the chances I never had. And I'm not likely to get another

86

job now, am I? Your father—he said he'd not give me a reference, and I'd not blame him. No boss wants someone who's been caught stealing.'

'I don't understand.' Rona looked round the shabby sitting room.

'There's only us,' said Jeannie. 'So I want the best for them.'

'Your mother?'

'She died three years ago—it was TB, they said, but she was never strong.'

'And your father?' Rona felt she was being inquisitive, but she was anxious to know about the little family. 'Could he not, I mean, is he . . .?'

She didn't like to say the word *dead*, so instead she asked, 'Is he—gone?'

'I'll say he's gone. Disappeared when George was three months old and no-one's seen hair nor hide of him since. Probably dead,' added Jeannie casually.

'Jeannie . . .' Rona didn't know how to put it. This poor little room, the family struggling for a living. 'Could you not get help—from the council? An allowance or something?'

'Me? I'm not going cap in hand to anyone. A woman came,' Jeannie added, 'wanting to know all about us. I soon shut her up.

'I never asked you to sit down,' she said as an afterthought. 'Take a chair.'

Rona perched uncomfortably on one of the dining chairs. She felt silenced, and astonished, too, that the meek little assistant should be so strong and determined, and not the least inclined to ask for pity.

'I'm not wanting pity,' said Jeannie suddenly as if she had read Rona's thoughts. 'I was caught stealing and that was it. Your father was right to sack me. So there's nothing more to be said.'

Rona's head was in a whirl. Why didn't I know, she asked herself, what was going on?

What a struggle Jeannie must have had those past three years, trying to bring up a family, and she was only, what, 16 or 17. Suddenly, Rona felt ashamed.

I've nothing to complain about, she thought. Oh, Aunt Lizzie is difficult to live with, and Father can be strict, but I don't have anything like Jeannie's problems. Thank heavens.

'Jeannie,' she said, 'how would it be if I spoke to my father?'

'Asked him to take me back, you mean? That's not likely, is it?' said the girl sharply.

'No,' Rona admitted. She knew how firm Angus could be, and how rigid in his attitudes.

He wasn't likely to change his mind out of pity for Jeannie and her family.

'I wish,' she said, 'there was something I could do to help.'

'There's nothing,' said Jeannie. 'But it's kind of you to try.'

Rona thought how changed Jeannie was. At work she had been self-effacing, hardly saying a word unless she was spoken to. Here she was in charge of the household and coping single-handed with two brothers, one it seemed, an invalid.

'I can't promise anything,' she said, 'but I'll do what I can.' She looked round the bare living room that shone all the same with cleanliness, and felt ashamed. This loyal, hard-working girl had been tempted to steal—whose fault was that, thought Rona with a spurt of anger.

'Is there anything you need?' she asked.

'Nothing.' Jeannie shook her head. 'I'd best finish the step. I like it to look clean for the morning.'

## A SECOND CHANCE

'You were a while in there,' said Callum. He was sitting placidly on a bollard, watching a fishing boat unload.

'I'm sorry,' Rona apologised.

'So what was that all about?' he asked.

'I'm sorry, I can't tell you. It's sort of private.'

All right.' He looked a little surprised but didn't press her further. 'Come on, let's go out the sands and up the hill.' He caught her hand.

She smiled at him. Callum was understanding, but it wasn't her secret to tell.

However, Rona decided, tomorrow she would talk to her father, first thing. Something surely could be done for Jeannie and her brothers.

*     *     *

'No, definitely not.' Rona recognised that tone. It meant that Angus refused to listen. He had made up his mind and that was that.

Rona talked to her friend, Nancy. 'Is your father like that? Stubborn?'

'He certainly is?' Nancy grimaced. She held out a crimson-tipped fingernail for Rona to inspect. 'What do you think of that colour?'

Rona was hardly listening. 'Oh yes, very nice?'

'Is that all? It's the newest shade.'

'Yes, it's lovely.' But Rona couldn't concentrate. 'If I asked him as a favour to do something to help someone who was very poorly off, you would think he'd agree, wouldn't you?'

'I don't know,' said Nancy cautiously. 'It depends on the person, I suppose. What do you want him to do?'

Rona was silent. Then she said, 'I'm sorry, it's rather private, about the person I mean. I'd be betraying a confidence if I told you.'

Nancy shrugged. 'Then I'm sorry I can't help. Your father must be as bad as mine. All I said was, "Can I go on holiday to a holiday camp?" and he refused, point blank. Said I wasn't to be trusted on my own. Me? I'm twenty-one, for goodness' sake. I could be married.' She sighed.

'What if . . .' Rona had a brilliant idea. 'What if someone was to go with you? A friend.'

'That might be different. If it was someone sensible.'

'Like me,' said Rona.

Nancy jumped up. 'What a wonderful idea! Ask your father, won't you? Tell him we'll be company for each other, and I'm a very responsible sort of person.' She grinned and put on what was supposed to be a sober expression.

'I'll do what I can,' said Rona.

But uppermost in her mind was the problem of Jeannie. She had told Jeannie she would do what she could to make Angus change his mind, but it seemed very unlikely that he would listen.

'No, certainly not,' he said firmly.

'But Father, if you could see that house—they're so poor and no mother or father.'

'Aye, I'm sure it's very pathetic, but that's no excuse for stealing.'

'But it was to buy boots for the older boy,' Rona protested. 'He needs them for school.'

'Maybe so,' said Angus. 'It's all very well pitching me a hard-luck story. It doesn't alter things. There're grants and allowances for people who are hard up,' he added. 'Now, as we're short-handed, you can wipe out the display case.'

Rona did so, glaring at him behind his back. But Angus was troubled. How like her mother Rona had become—the same soft heart, and desperate to help anyone down on their luck.

The same wide generosity for everyone, no matter what their faults. And maybe, he thought, maybe this girl, Jeannie, was doing her best to keep the family together. Of course he couldn't have Jeannie back, he couldn't employ anyone untrustworthy. But there might be another way.

\*       \*       \*

Rona still felt anxious about Doug. 'But its not my problem,' she told herself. 'If he was stupid enough to get embroiled with that Neela, it was his own fault.'

However, she didn't like to see her brother so down. He would sit at the table with a blank expression, eating whatever Rona had cooked without comment.

'You might say something,' she burst out one evening.

'Say what?' he looked at her blankly.

'Well, you could say you enjoyed the meal.' She had taken particular trouble over the fish pie.

'Yeah, it's fine.'

Rona gave up. If he wanted to sulk, let him.

'I'm away out,' he said.

Please yourself. Rona began to gather up the dishes.

Despite the coolness between them, she couldn't help feeling worried about Doug. He was normally so easy-going and cheerful. It wasn't like him to be grumpy as he had been for the past month or so.

Oh, that girl! she thought. Why did he ever get involved with her?

Meantime, Callum and Rona had become good friends—she enjoyed his sense of humour, and their evenings out—sometimes a walk, sometimes sharing a bag of pan drops at the pictures, and usually once a week at the ceilidh at the town hall. Rona beamed at him as he swung her round in the Gay Gordons and he thought how pretty she was, with that golden hair and her blue eyes that sparkled with fun.

As they sat in the balcony, sipping lemonade, he turned to her. 'I wondered,' he said, 'if you'd like to come up to the farm one afternoon—maybe have your tea with us.'

'I'd like that.' She had been wondering when Callum was going to invite her to his home to meet his family.

Of course, it wasn't easy to ask him to her home, not with Doug in a mood, and Father saying very little. Then there was Aunt Lizzie—she'd be coming back next week, and

Rona knew how Callum dreaded meeting her in the shop. It wouldn't be any easier at home.

'Maybe next Saturday?'

Rona nodded. He put an arm round her. 'You're a lovely girl, do you know that? I've met a lot of girls, taken a few out, but there's not been anyone special. Not until now.'

He bent his head and drew her close. He was about to kiss her when the mood was shattered.

'Would you look at that?' Rona gasped.

Callum, slightly annoyed that the romantic moment had been spoiled, said, 'What's the matter?'

'Nothing,' said Rona leaning over the balcony. 'But you see that boy dancing the eightsome—see him in the centre?'

Drawing attention to himself, thought Callum a little sourly as he watched the figure, his arms raised and uttering joyful whoops.

'So what?'

'It's Doug,' said Rona. 'Well, he's certainly recovered. I'd no idea he was coming to the ceilidh. And there's no sign of Neela.'

'Rona . . .' Callum caught her arm. 'I was saying . . .'

'Come on, let's go downstairs,' said Rona. 'I want a word with him,' she said grimly.

He sighed and followed her down the stairs to the hall where the eightsome had just ended.

'Well, I didn't expect to see you here.' Rona

94

stood four-square in front of her brother.

He looked a little shame-faced.

'And where's Neela?' asked Rona.

'I told you. I'm not seeing her again.' He caught the arm of a tall, dark-haired girl.

'This is Bet . . . she's the best dancer in the hall.'

'Och, you—' she gave him a little push that made him rock back on his heels. 'He's an awful one, this Doug. Come on, it's the ladies' choice and I'm drouthy. I'm wanting a drink of lemonade before the next dance.'

Doug grinned apologetically at Rona.

'I think we can say,' said Rona slowly, 'that he's got over Neela. It certainly looks as if he's back to normal.' And she added grimly, 'From now on he gets no sympathy from me, and he can take his turn doing the dishes.'

It was about a week later—she was at the bus station to collect some parcels when her eye was caught by a slim, elegant figure.

She wore a smart full-skirted coat and a little black hat with a veil, perched on her curls. She seemed to have a number of suitcases.

She stood smoking a cigarette through a long black holder and very much aware that a number of people were looking at her. Suddenly, Rona knew who she was.

'You're Neela, aren't you?' She went up to the girl.

'And if I am?' The girl blew a couple of

smoke rings.

'I'm Doug's sister.'

'Doug?' Neela looked puzzled.

'Don't pretend you don't know who he was. You crashed your brother's car when Doug was teaching you to drive.'

'Oh, Doug?' Neela said, as if suddenly remembering. 'A nice boy. Not many nice young men around this place.'

'You broke his heart,' said Rona sternly, but then she thought, that wasn't really true.

Remembering Doug whooping and swinging his partner at the ceilidh, she couldn't honestly say he was broken-hearted.

'Can I help it,' said Neela, 'if men fall for me? He was a nice boy, your brother, but a bit young for me. I like my men sophisticated. Anyway,' she added, 'I'm away from this dump. Back to the bright lights for me, and a bit of real life.'

Just then the bus arrived and she climbed in, with a brief nod towards a young man who hurried forward to help her with her cases.

'Have you got a message for Doug?' Rona called.

'No, not really. Bye . . .' and she was gone.

\*     \*     \*


'I saw the mysterious Neela,' Rona told Callum the next evening. 'Getting on a bus, to go back to the bright lights, she said.'

96

'Is that so?' Callum's eyes twinkled, and he gave a guffaw of laughter.

'Bright lights.' He rocked backwards and forwards.

'I can't see what's so funny,' said Rona stiffly.

'Don't you know?' he said. 'Her folks have the farm over at Northlea. She came home for a bit—she's been living off her parents, but they got fed up with her and they've thrown her out.'

'I didn't know.'

'Everyone else did,' said Callum. 'She couldn't hold down a job in Edinburgh—walked out of ever so many. She was a mother's help—I doubt she'd be any good at that.'

'But she was so—glamorous,' said Rona. 'I thought she must be an actress or a model maybe.'

'Not her. Her dad said she spent all her time at the pictures—that's where she picked up the grand manner. He made her get a job—she worked in the laundry, but she's left that job. Away back to Edinburgh, you said?'

'I saw her at the bus station. And as for her clothes,' said Rona, 'she must have plenty of money.'

'Well,' Callum hesitated. 'Not to gossip, but she did have a number of boyfriends—some of them well-heeled, by the sound of it. I reckon that's the last we'll see of her.'

Rona decided then, that Doug was obviously over the glamorous Neela and had moved on. He'd been young and had his head easily turned, but was now back to his usual self.

She thought of that wild figure on the dance floor, flinging himself and his partner about, and she grinned. Somehow she felt the love-sick Doug was very definitely cured.

*　　　*　　　*

When she got home that evening, Angus was sitting in his favourite chair by the fireside.

The fire was lit, as the evening had become chilly and he held out his hands to the blaze in the grate.

'That you, Rona?'

'It's me.' She took off her coat. 'You're up later tonight.'

'I've been thinking—and talking to a few folk. That girl, Jeannie . .'

'Yes?'

'Maybe,' he said tapping the ash out of his pipe, 'maybe you were right. Maybe she should get a second chance.'

'Father!'

'I'm not taking her back, mind,' he said hastily 'But I've been talking to Miss Nairn at the school and she'd be prepared to take Jeannie on as a cleaner, and maybe a job in the school kitchen. So you can tell her, she's to go up there, Monday, after four o'clock, and Miss Nairn will see her. She'll have to behave, mind, and any sign she's light-fingered, she'll be up in the Sheriff Court.'

'Oh, Father!' Rona was overjoyed. 'I know she won't let you down.'

'She'd better not. Well, I'm away to my bed.'

Angus turned away. The way her face lit up when she was happy, and her sudden smile— Rona was so like her mother, he thought with a sigh.


## AUNT LIZZIE RETURNS

'Your aunt Lizzie says Maisie's a lot better,' said Angus, scanning the letter he held.

'Lizzie will be coming home in about ten days' time.'

Doug looked up from his plate of porridge. 'So we've ten days left of freedom?'

Rona was pleased to see that he had recovered his spirits. He spent a lot of his free time at the football pitch with some of his friends, and there had been no more mention of Neela.

Angus looked at him reprovingly. 'That's no way to talk of your aunt,' he said. But he added, 'We'll be pleased to see her back, of course. Not that you haven't done a grand job,' he told Rona.

Rona beamed. Her father was slow to praise, but she knew she'd done her best. Never mind that the grate wasn't black-leaded the way Aunt Lizzie kept it or that her ironing was slap-dash, and the windows could do with a good clean.

Rona wouldn't admit it to anyone, but she too would be quite glad to see Aunt Lizzie back. She could be bossy and overbearing, but she ran the house like clockwork. Even though life had been more easy-going without her, Rona knew they couldn't have managed without Aunt Lizzie since Mother had died. Oh, wouldn't it be a relief not to have to toil away at housework, especially in these lovely summer evenings.

I wish I could have a holiday, she thought as she made her way home after an evening out with Callum.

As she pushed open the front door, Rona heard a familiar voice.

'And here you are—where do you think you've been till this time of night?'

'Aunt Lizzie—you're back!'

Her aunt was setting the table for breakfast.

'I got back earlier this evening. Your father's away to his bed, and Doug—he'll be out somewhere.'

'It's good to have you back.' Somehow Aunt Lizzie looked right, there in the kitchen.

'Well, I can tell you, I'm not sorry to be back. Except that . . .' Aunt Lizzie didn't finish

100

the sentence and Rona wondered what she had been going to say.

Rona realised that she was tired. It had been a busy spell with Aunt Lizzie away and being short-handed in the shop. Still, Angus had been true to his word. He had gone along to the Labour Exchange and hired a new assistant.

Elsie had recently left school and was full of enthusiasm. 'My, you're lucky to have a father who's a baker,' she told Rona. 'What a grand job—working here all the time.'

She dabbed up a few crumbs of a fruit scone. 'If I couldn't work in a sweetie shop, I'd choose to work in a baker's.'

She was a cheerful sort of girl, and sang as she went about her work. 'I'll just have a wee taste,' she would say, and Rona began to be alarmed that her new assistant seemed to be tasting a great deal.

'You'd better not let my father catch you, or Aunt Lizzie,' she said with a glance towards the cash desk.

'But I thought,' began Elsie, 'it's like a sweetie shop. They let you try everything for the first few days, until you're sick and don't want to eat any more.'

'It's not like that here,' said Rona firmly.

'Oh well, maybe Mr Maclaren would give me a few stale cakes at the end of the day?' she said hopefully. 'I'll not mind if they're a bit hard.'

'Well,' Rona was doubtful. But she had to admit that the customers liked Elsie and her enthusiasm.

'You've not tried the pancakes,' she would say in a confidential tone, leaning over the counter. 'Just the thing for your tea.'

And the customer, who had not thought till now, of buying pancakes, found herself going out of the shop with pancakes and scones as well as the tea bread she had come in to buy.

But, despite the extra hand in the shop, and Aunt Lizzie's return, Rona began to feel extra tired and out of sorts.

Once or twice she had snapped at Callum, and her friend, Nancy, looked at her sternly. 'You're needing a holiday,' she said. 'Why don't we go away, us two. I've a week due me in August.'

She went on, 'I've never been to a holiday camp. What about it? There's dancing every night—it would be great fun. You never know who we'd meet.' She grinned, then she looked serious. 'You'd never catch my father letting me go. But if I went with you?'

Rona's face brightened. 'That would be wonderful,' she said. Her mind drifted towards a week of sunny days and lazing around the swimming pool and waltzing in the ballroom every evening—and maybe walks under the stars with someone.

'Hey,' said Nancy, 'wake up. What about it?'

'I'll ask Father,' Rona promised. 'But I don't

expect him to agree. His idea of a holiday is a few days in a caravan in the rain, if you're lucky. Or a stay at Aunt Maisie's where there's no-one under sixty.' She looked gloomy. 'But I'll try it anyway.'

Meanwhile, things were going well for Angus. The business was thriving, Rona had worked hard, and the new girl—well, she seemed to be settling down.

And the whole town of Kirkton, in fact the whole country, was agog. For it wasn't long till the Coronation, the crowning of the new Queen, Elizabeth II.

## AN ENTERPRISING IDEA

'So, Mr Maclaren. We'll confirm the numbers early in the week. All the primary children and maybe a few bags over just to be on the safe side. I don't think,' smiled Miss Jessop, 'we'll have many absentees that day.'

'A grand occasion—the Coronation parade—and you may be sure we'll do you proud.'

'I'm sure you will, Mr Maclaren,' said the deputy headmistress. 'After all, it's not every day we have the crowning of a queen.'

'Just so.' Angus held open the door for her. 'Good day to you.'

'That's a good order,' he told Rona later.

103

'The bairns get their bags when they've marched along the High Street and down to the park. Sausage rolls, scones, iced buns, and they'll get a drink of lemonade and an ice-cream. Oh, it's going to be a grand day. I just hope it keeps fine.'

Father was in a good mood today, thought Rona. For months, there had been growing excitement about the crowning of the new Queen.

There were souvenir mugs and tea towels, and biscuit tins. There was to be a Coronation parade with all the school children waving flags and finishing up in the park for their tea.

Some people had bought or hired television sets for the great day, June 2nd, and were arranging parties for families and friends, to crowd round the set and watch the flickering black and white scenes from Westminster Abbey.

The shop across the road from the baker's that sold wireless sets had a larger television set and a few old folk had been invited in to watch the event.

Aunt Lizzie was eager to see the Coronation on the screen. 'I think I'll have to listen on the wireless, and go and see it when they show it at the picture house,' she said. Meantime, she contented herself with reading everything she could about the event.

'It would be grand to be there,' she said wistfully. 'I wouldn't even mind sleeping out in

104

the Mall, seeing all the flags, and waiting for the procession.'

Rona smiled to herself. Since Aunt Lizzie had returned she was a little quieter, not so sharp-tongued. There had even been the occasional word of praise for Rona's efforts.

And who would have thought that Aunt Lizzie would become so sentimental over a Royal occasion?

Angus—now he wasn't one for display. However, there was no harm in asking.

'Father,' Rona said, hesitantly, 'do you think I could decorate our window, just for the Coronation?'

'Ah, well,' said Angus slowly. 'We're not needing to. Folk won't stop buying pan loaves and tattie scones. They'll come to the shop anyway.'

'But everyone else is going to have a window display,' Rona protested. 'Gibson's the ironmonger, and the toy shop and the bookseller, and Miss Douglas at the haberdasher's.'

'Well, if you like,' he conceded. 'But mind and keep it tasteful. And don't go spending a lot of money,' he added.

'Oh, thank you,' said Rona. 'Could I get some money for ribbons, and that sort of thing?'

A little reluctantly, Angus agreed.

Rona started happily making plans. Oh, she would keep it simple, but colourful, she decided.

She raided Aunt Lizzie's collection of pictures of the young Queen, and bought as many yards of red, white and blue ribbon as she could afford.

She spent an evening tracing the outline of a crown on to paper, then laboriously cut it out in cardboard and covered the cardboard with gold paper she'd bought from the stationer. With the aid of a school compass she'd long put away in a cupboard, she made star shapes, cut out the stars and covered them too in gold.

The Queen's picture was pasted on to a piece of card and edged with gold braid Rona had begged from Aunt Lizzie's workbox.

But it needed something extra, she thought, as she started to decorate the window.

'It looks grand,' said Callum loyally.

But Rona was not satisfied. 'It needs, I don't know—something special—I mean a link to us, to the baker's,' she said, wishing that Father had agreed to produce shortbread in Coronation tins.

'You should enter for the competition,' said one customer, as she watched Rona crawling about the window. 'You get the forms at the town hall, and the Provost's judging.'

Rona looked thoughtful, and in her lunch hour she went along to the town hall and completed the form. She would tell Father later.

On the way back, she gazed into some of

the window displays. The ironmonger had scrubbing brushes and shiny metal pails surrounding a picture of the young Queen.

'I doubt she'll need to scrub her own floors,' thought Rona with a grin.

The stationer's had display of books about the Royal family, postcards and photographs. Nearly everyone had ribbons and bunting and Royal pictures.

The window Rona liked best was the toy shop across the way. A toy train chugged across the back of the window and at each side stood wooden soldiers painted in red, white and blue. At the front of the window were three teddy bears, wearing red white and blue bows, with their paws raised in salute.

The baker's window looked bright, thought Rona, but somehow there was nothing special that would catch the eye of the judges. 'Father,' she said, 'do you think I could have some shortbread biscuits and ice them?'

He looked doubtful. Then, 'Just a few,' he said. 'This'll be for your window?'

'Yes, please.'

Angus didn't say anything else—he was secretly quite proud of Rona ever since one or two customers had commented on the window.

Rona spent a long time after work getting the icing to just the right consistency, and setting out the piping tubes she wanted to use.

She thought for a bit what message she should choose. *Loyal Greetings*—that would take a great deal of effort, and quite a few biscuits. She would have liked to have written, *Long live the Queen*, or *Elizabeth II*, but she discarded these ideas.

Finally she got out one of the silver bases that were used for wedding and birthday cakes so that she could fix the biscuits on to the base. Finally, she decided to keep it simple.

She piped the letters laboriously, trying to keep her hand steady as she'd watched her father when he was decorating a cake.

She waited till the icing had dried, then secured the biscuits to the base and placed it carefully in front of the window.

It was simple, she thought, and effective and it said what everyone thought about the Coronation and the new Queen.

Well, now, she thought, she had done her best—she would just have to wait for the judges' decision.

Quite a few people stopped to admire the window.

'Your lassie's done a good job,' said one woman to Angus. 'Makes a fair difference to your window.'

'Aye.' Angus was reluctant to admit it, but it had been good for business. Customers kept coming into the shop, asking for the Coronation biscuits. 'We'll have a few more of these,' he said to Rona. 'Folk seem to like the iced biscuits.' So he produced a batch with *EIIR* and a few with crowns. 'They're selling like hot cakes,' he said to Lizzie with a rare attempt of humour. 'Not a bad idea of Rona's.'

## A DAY OF CELEBRATION

Two days before the Coronation, the judges came round. Rona watched from inside the shop at the two men who stood in front of the window with notepads. She wished she could see what they were writing. A *Highly Commended* would be nice, a third or a second even better.

Next day the awards were announced. As Rona had expected, the toy shop got first prize. Well, she told herself what else? Those bears with their red, white and blue bows were really appealing. Every day there had been crowds of small children oohing and aahing in front of the window until they were dragged away by their mothers.

But then, the girl from the town clerk's office popped her head round the door, as she waved a card. 'Second prize, Mr Maclaren,' she called out. 'Well done!'

'Well done, Rona,' said Angus. 'It was a bright idea of yours, and its done our business no harm, no harm at all. Away you go and put the card in the window, and I'd better see about some more of these biscuits.'

'You've put Maclaren's on the map,' said

Callum later. 'I'm really proud of you.'

Aunt Lizzie didn't say very much except, 'We should have had Coronation shortbread tins. I told Angus.'

'You told him no such thing,' said Rona under her breath. But she didn't want to spoil this special day by arguing with Aunt Lizzie, who really, thought Rona, was much better-tempered since her return.

Now Aunt Lizzie was keeping an eye on the wireless shop across the road. 'Mrs McFarlane tells me the owner's having a lot of old folk in to watch the television,' she said. I wonder . . .' she turned to Angus. 'It would be a kindly gesture if you were to give them a slab of sultana cake for their tea.'

'I never heard the like. You'll have me bankrupt.' He pretended to be stern, but Rona knew him well enough. Father would agree.

'Oh, Father,' Rona protested. 'It's the Coronation—it's a special occasion.'

'Ah, well,' he said. 'Maybe you're right. Away you go, Lizzie, and take them a couple of slabs of sultana cake.'

Aunt Lizzie returned from her errand, beaming. Rona couldn't remember when she had last seen her aunt looking so pleased about anything.

'He said to thank you kindly,' she reported to Angus, 'and the old folk will enjoy the cake. And he's asked me if I'd like to go across—if we're not busy here—and watch the ceremony

110

on the television. Fancy that! I'll see the Queen being crowned!'

*     *     *

It was certainly a day to remember. There was the news that Mount Everest had been climbed—the news came over the wireless that Hillary and Tenzing had reached the summit.

'A grand beginning to Her Majesty's reign,' said Angus.

Aunt Lizzie watched the ceremony throughout—the arrival of the young Queen with her maids of honour and the Queen Mother and Princess Margaret watching from above with a young Prince Charles.

The solemn moments of the anointing, Prince Philip taking the oath of loyalty to the Queen—there were so many memorable moments.

Outside Westminster Abbey, the crowds ignored the rain. Some had been waiting all night in the Mall, sharing sandwiches and flasks of tea and joking with the policemen on duty.

Even in Kirkton there were so many memories of that day. The sound of the town band, the children waving their flags, marching to the park: Running off their energy in sack races and egg and spoon races, before they queued for lemonade and paper bags containing sandwiches and iced buns.

111

When they'd finished eating, some of them blew up the bags  when they'd finished and burst them. It was a grand day that finished with three cheers for the Queen.

'And let's have three cheers for Mr Maclaren who gave us the buns and cakes,' one of the organisers announced. The children roared themselves hoarse. It had been a great day.

Things were all rather flat when Coronation day was over —except that everyone would be going to the Regal when the film of the Coronation reached the cinemas.

Rona felt particularly flat. It was fun going out with Callum, but it had become a bit of a routine—a walk along the shore, a coffee in the local café, to watch the TV the owner had just lately installed.

Saturday nights meant queuing for the pictures or maybe going to a dance at the town hall. There was, she thought, no glamour, no exciting romance.

'I'm only young,' she said to herself rebelliously. 'Why shouldn't I have a bit of romance?'

She wished she could meet someone—he needn't be tall, dark and handsome, though it would be nice if he was. No, she'd settle for someone who looked into her eyes as if she were the only girl in the world.

Callum, stocky, fair-haired and with a ready laugh, was good company, but that was all.

Surely there was more to life than this.

And suddenly, she felt tired, bored with the daily grind. 'I need a holiday,' she said, and remembered what Nancy had suggested.

'A holiday camp!' That was it. Lots of fun, dancing every night, meeting new people.

She would put it to her father.

'I'd like a holiday, just a week.'

'Oh well, aye,' said Angus pausing in his work. 'I suppose you're due it. And we could manage fine for a week. You'll be going away I suppose, maybe to your Auntie Cassie?'

Rona shuddered. Auntie Cassie lived in the suburbs of Edinburgh—staid and grey-haired, she was kindly, but oh so dull!

She never went to a film or a theatre, or trailed round the shops. She had never been to the Castle or Holyrood or the Botanic Gardens, and saw no reason why Rona should wish to visit any of these places.

Rona had stayed there once before and discovered Auntie Cassie's main interest was family history. How many photograph albums she'd put in front of Rona, she couldn't remember.

'This was my great aunt—you'll not remember her. And here's Uncle Hamish—he was a great character.'

It was hard to see from the grim-looking figures staring into the camera, how any of them had been fun, or had kicked over the traces when they were young. No, a visit to

Aunt Cassie was not Rona's idea of a holiday.

'Oh no,' she said. 'I'd like to go to a holiday camp.'

'A holiday camp!' Angus's voice rose. 'That you will not.'

'Oh, Father. This is nineteen fifty-three. Lots of people go to holiday camps. You can have a great week.'

'I'm not having you going off to a holiday camp. I don't know what you'd get up to.'

Rona sighed. 'I'd be going with Nancy.'

Angus hesitated. 'Oh, aye.' He knew Nancy's parents—sensible folk, her father an elder of the church, and Nancy herself had a good position in the council offices. She was sure to be a restraining influence on Rona.

'Please, Father,' said Rona.

He looked at his daughter's bright face and knew how disappointed she would be if he refused permission. After all, it was only a week, and she would be with Nancy.

'Oh, all right then.'

'Thank you!' Rona beamed. 'The first week in August—is that all right? Nancy's office is closed then.'

'You've got it all planned, I see.' He shook his head. 'Well, then you can have your holiday.'

He turned and lifted a tray of potato scones. 'Now don't waste my time—there's these shelves to be wiped.'

# A DIFFICULT VISIT

'Great!' said Nancy when she heard that Angus had agreed to Rona going to the holiday camp. 'As long as I'm with you,' said Rona with a smile. 'He thinks you're a responsible person.'

'Just what my dad said about you.'

The two girls fell about laughing. Then Nancy sat up and wiped her eyes.

'Let's be serious. I'll arrange the booking and we must decide on clothes for the holiday. Have you got a swimsuit? No? Then we'll have a trip to Dundee, the next half day.'

'It won't be long now,' said Rona. 'Oh I am looking forward to it all . . .'

*         *         *

Rona had been made a welcome visitor to Callum's home. She'd been invited one Sunday.

'Just a cup of tea, don't dress up,' Callum had warned her. 'And don't pay any attention to what my mother says.'

Rona had been a little apprehensive about this. Would his mother be difficult, very critical perhaps?

She didn't mention the visit at home. By now Aunt Lizzie was back in her usual place, though somehow she didn't seem as irritating as before. Lips pursed, she had given the floor a good clean.

'It looks as if it hasn't been washed since I left,' she had said grimly. Rona had been about to snap back at her, 'Do you think I had nothing else to do?' but she had held her tongue. I must be growing up, she thought.

Still, Aunt Lizzie had looked at the cupboards, and given a nod of approval. 'Tidy, I will say.' But Rona knew this was Aunt Lizzie's way of giving praise.

So now, she wondered what to wear for the visit to the farm. Not her Sunday best dress— that would be too formal. Besides, Callum had promised to show her round, and not her best shoes, those with the little heels—she'd saved for those and they were far too smart to waste on a visit to the farm.

At last she decided on a light wool skirt, and a pretty turquoise blue jumper that Aunt Lizzie had knitted for her.

\*      \*      \*

Callum's mother had been busy at the cooker when they arrived. 'Well, here you are!' she greeted them.

She was a little woman, hardly coming up to Callum's shoulder, with a round rosy face and her hair piled up on top of her head. She'd wiped her hands on a cloth, and shaken hands with Rona.

116

'So!' she had looked Rona up and down. 'I've been at him to bring you up for your tea—and here you are at last. You're the first one he's ever brought home. I said to his father, "He must be serious about this one, our Callum".'

Rona had blushed and stammered something.

'Now,' Callum's mother had said, 'you don't need to stand on ceremony with us. We just have our tea in the kitchen—maybe on a very special occasion we use the parlour. You'll not mind the kitchen,' she'd run on, not waiting for an answer. 'If I've asked him once, I've asked him twenty times—what's wrong with the lass that you don't bring her to see us?'

She'd paused for breath and Callum, by now shining uncomfortably had said, 'Now, Mother, that's enough. You'll embarrass Rona.'

He'd then said hastily, 'I'll take Rona out to look round for a bit, and we'll come back for our tea.'

'Your father and the boys will be back for five,' his mother had said.

Outside, there had been a constraint between Callum and Rona.

'Come on,' he'd said, 'I told you not to pay any attention to what my mother says. She's always like that.'

Rona had frowned. 'She said that you'd never brought a girl back home before.' She hesitated. 'I don't want your family to get the wrong idea about us.'

'Don't be daft,' he'd said. 'What is there to get ideas about?'

Rona had felt vaguely disappointed. Well, they were just friends, after all, but he had made it perfectly clear there was nothing else.

He'd dismissed out of hand the idea that there was any romance between them. And of course, he was quite right.

I don't know what I want, that's my trouble, she thought. Maybe a break away from each other is a good idea

He helped her over a stile and she jumped down on the other side.

'Look,' he said, 'you can see for miles.' They looked down over the fields to the main road away in the distance and the little cars that looked like toys. Far away you could see the Firth of Forth and the small villages strung out along the coastline.

They leaned against the stile, and Callum put his arm around her as he pointed out other farms and white-washed houses.

'I hope it's weather like this when we're on holiday.' She'd hesitated about telling Callum of her holiday plans—somehow she thought he might not take too kindly to the idea. 'Nancy and I—we're having a week at a holiday camp. At the beginning of August,' she added. 'It should be fun.'

'Oh?' Callum sounded surprised, and

118

Rona's heart sank. She burbled on, 'Dancing every night and swimming and all sorts of entertainment. It should be great.'

'Oh . . .' he was silent for a few moments then he said, 'Well, I hope you have a good time. I'd thought, maybe after the harvest you and I could go hostelling, hire bikes, perhaps. But if you've already made plans . . .'

'I'm sorry,' said Rona, though she didn't quite know why she was apologising. 'But I know farmers don't often get holidays.'

'I could,' said Callum. 'There's my father and brothers here. I could get away.'

'Oh, well,' said Rona airily, 'too late now.'

'I'm sure you'll have a wonderful time,' he said a little stiffly. Suddenly Rona was irritated. 'I'm sure we will. Sorry about the hostelling, but I don't know if it would suit me.'

As you've already made your plans anyway . . .' he began.

'Callum!' Rona burst out. 'You don't own me, you know. I've a perfect right to go on holiday with someone else.' She was still a little upset by his easy dismissal of their friendship as nothing to get ideas about.

'I thought we were friends, but . . .' he said.

'Of course we are!' said Rona quickly. Oh, why did the argument have to happen here? Now she'd have to go back to the farmhouse for tea, pretending that all was well.

'But I think,' she added, 'that perhaps we've

119

been seeing too much of each other. Maybe we should have a little break.'

'Come on,' he said, 'it's time we went back. My mother will have the tea on the table.'

Suddenly the summer's day was spoiled for Rona. What had happened to their easy friendship full of fun and laughter? Now they were like strangers to each other—like people who had only just met. What had happened to those light-hearted months they'd shared?

Callum was silent as he had led the way back to the farmhouse.

'Sit in, and make a good tea,' Callum's mother told her. His father, a large, cheerful man, rather like an older version of Callum, rose from his seat.

'So this is Rona,' he said, grasping her hand in his huge grip. 'Pleased to meet you.'

The two brothers nodded shyly and made room for her at the table.

'Can I help you carrying things through?' Rona asked.

'No, no, lassie. You sit there.' Mrs Scott waved away Rona's offer. 'But it's nice of you to want to help.'

It was a real farmhouse high tea—a steak pie, followed by scones and fruit loaf and a sponge cake fresh from the oven, with a strong brew of tea.

Rona tried to eat everything, but she found she had little appetite, and glancing across at Callum, saw that he wasn't eating much either.

'You've an awful wee appetite,' Mrs Scott ('Call me Jess') said cheerily. 'My, but we'll soon put a bit of weight on you.'

She was eager to know about Rona's family, though of course most people on the district knew Maclaren's the baker's, and how he'd lost his wife when Rona was still at school, and how Aunt Lizzie had come to look after them all, and how she'd been away lately helping her sister-in-law.

'You'll be used to running a house,' said Jess approvingly, as Rona helped to clear the table.

Callum's father, who had been silent for most of the time, became more talkative as he showed Rona the stable, the byre, and the barn where the dogs greeted her.

'Get down!' he told them. 'See this one, Fly, Callum's brother, Bob, is training him. We're hoping to enter him for the trials. He's doing well, he was the best of the litter.'

Rona liked Callum's father, and his bright, bustling little mother. It would have been good to get to know the brothers who were both silent and looked at her warily, but had shaken her by the hand and muttered a greeting.

But Callum was a little distant—there was still this awkwardness between them. She thought, 'I deserve a holiday. And why not? It isn't as if we were engaged or anything.'

'I'll run you back,' he said.

'There's no need.'

'Father lets me have the van sometimes if I need it.'

'Thank you,' she said formally.

As he dropped her at the house, she said again, 'I enjoyed the afternoon, and meeting your family.'

She remembered Jess's words, as she said goodbye. 'Now you'll come and see us again soon, mind.'

But she did wonder if she would be visiting the farm again—ever.


## A DREAM HOLIDAY

Rona missed Callum's visits to the shop, and their weekly trips to the pictures or the café. But it was a good idea, she told herself, to have a break.

Their relationship had become a matter of routine. 'We had got used to each other,' she decided. 'There was no excitement, and there weren't any surprises about our friendship.' Maybe he would meet someone else. And she'd be glad for him.

Anyway, there was enough to think about— the holiday to plan for, and it was a hectic time in the shop now that the holidaymakers had arrived.

Angus was kept busy baking rolls and pies for the people in the holiday homes and caravans.

Rona couldn't help feeling a little guilty about going away just at this time. 'Are you sure you'll manage without me?' she asked her father anxiously.

'Of course we will. And your Aunt Lizzie's here to help,' he said.

That was another thing. Aunt Lizzie had been in rather a strange mood since she returned from helping Maisie. Rona couldn't understand it.

Sometimes her aunt seemed quite remote, as if she were thinking of something else entirely. And she was quieter too —she didn't snap at Doug and Rona the way she used to, and she seemed somehow less critical of Rona than she had been in the past.

'Have you noticed anything about her?' Rona asked her brother.

He shook his head. 'Can't say I have.'

That was just like Doug, Rona thought, exasperated. He never noticed anything about anyone. But if it was a matter of an odd sound in a car engine, or recognising a car number plate, that was a different matter.

Rona shrugged. No use asking Doug—and Father had enough to think about, but there was definitely something very strange about Aunt Lizzie. Could she be ill?

Rona tried to put her concern to one side. Aunt Lizzie was as busy as usual in the shop, and wouldn't have welcomed questions. 'When

I come back from holiday,' Rona promised herself, 'I'll try to find out what's the matter.'

She couldn't wait for the week's holiday. Together the two girls had made a shopping trip to Dundee, where Rona had bought a bright blue one-piece swimsuit.

'I've never had anything so smart,' she said gleefully. 'It's so much nicer than that old ruched bathing suit I've had for ages.'

She splashed out, too, on a pair of peep-toed sandals. 'Only a week to go,' she said, counting.

\*       \*       \*

Right from the first day, the holiday was all they'd expected. Queuing with other campers at a long desk to pay for their week's hoard, Rona felt that the holiday had really begun as they were handed the keys of their chalet.

'It doesn't really matter if it rains,' said Nancy, looking at the programme, 'there's so much to do.'

But it didn't rain. Each day seemed sunnier than the last. There was tennis, and swimming, and entertainment, it seemed round the clock, and in the evenings the ballroom was turned into quite a magical place, with fairy lights and a wonderful band playing the very latest tunes.

The girls soon met up with other holidaymakers of their own age and there was no shortage of partners at the dances. And of course all the time, the entertainment staff were on hand to make sure that everyone enjoyed the holiday.

But it was in the mail room, an unlikely spot, that Rona met Jake.

She was buying stamps to send her postcards home when she turned and bumped into someone.

'Oh, sorry!'

'No need to apologise.' He was smartly dressed in a navy blazer with a neckerchief. His hair was slicked back and she caught a whiff of some pleasant after-shave.

'I've seen you around,' he said. 'Weren't you at the concert last night?'

And that was how it started. 'Perhaps you'll be going to the dance this evening?'

'My friend and I—we go dancing every night,' Rona said 'We're having such a good time.'

'Then I'll keep an eye out for you this evening,' he said with a smile.

As she left the mail room, having almost forgotten to stamp her cards and put them in the box, she glanced back and caught him looking after her.

'I met someone,' she told Nancy over lunch in the huge dining room.

'That's quick,' Nancy laughed.

'He's going to watch for us at tonight's dance,' said Rona.

'For you—you mean,' Nancy teased her.

'Well . . .' Rona blushed.

She knew she was looking her best that evening, in a crisp cotton dress—white printed with a pattern of small violets. She wore her new sandals and had made up carefully, with just a dusting of powder and a new Natural Rose lipstick. A quick spray of Chypre toilet water and she was ready.

'You do look nice,' said Nancy admiringly. 'So who's this in aid of?'

'No-one special,' said Rona firmly, but she did hope that the handsome stranger would be at the dance.

It was about half-way through the evening when he suddenly appeared at her side.

'Remember me? Would you like to dance? I'm Jake. And you are?'

'Rona.' She smiled at him. It was a quickstep—her favourite. He was a good dancer. Such a change, she thought from the young men she'd danced with up to now.

She'd winced as one trod on her toes, with a, 'Sorry, I'm not a very good dancer.'

Rona had smiled forgivingly. She'd keep out of his way in future.

But Jake, he was different. At the end of the dance, he took her back to the side of the hall. 'And the next dance?'

Rona hesitated. 'I'm with a friend,' she said.

'The girl in the green dress? You were standing together.'

'Yes, that's Nancy.'

'Well,' he said, 'you don't need to worry about her. It looks as if she's having a very good time.' He nodded towards a group where Nancy was at the centre, laughing and chatting.

'So, let's go and have a drink.'

'Lemonade, please, or orange squash,' Rona pushed back a lock of hair. 'I'm thirsty.'

'Wait there. I'll be back.'

She watched him making his way through the dancers, carrying two bottles of lemonade.

He was, she decided, the most handsome man she'd ever met—only medium height, but he had dark curling hair and in profile looked very like one of her favourite film stars, but she couldn't decide which one.

'Now,' he said, as he found them a couple of chairs, 'tell me how you're enjoying your holiday and what you've been doing.'

'Oh, everything,' she said happily. 'Playing tennis, swimming, watching all the competitions—the children's fancy dress to the knobbly knees contest.' She smiled. 'There never seems to be a moment to spare.'

'So it's your first time at the camp?'

Rona nodded. 'I'm so glad we came here.'

'I'm glad too.' He smiled at her. 'So tell me, Rona, where are you from and what do you do? No,' he held up a hand. 'Let me guess. You're maybe something in advertising, or you're a model? Yes that's it—you're a model.'

Rona shook her head. 'No, I'm not—though

127

I'd like to be.'

'So what's your line of business?'

Rona hesitated. 'I help in a family business.'

'I knew it,' he said. 'Bright as well as beautiful.'

Rona blushed. Why had she not said that she worked in the family baker's shop?

'And you?' she said hastily.

'Oh, I'm in the entertainment business.' he said. 'But let's talk about you. You really are most attractive.'

'I'd like to dance again.' Rona finished her lemonade.

'Then may I?' he said. 'Unless of course you've promised someone else.'

'Oh, no.'

Jake took her hand and led her on to the dance floor. 'We dance well together, don't we?'

From then on they danced every dance together, until the slow dreamy tune, *Goodnight, Campers*, signalled that the evening was over.

He put his arm round her as they walked back to her chalet. 'Listen, Rona,' he said, 'you mentioned you'd like to be a model.'

'Just a dream,' said Rona hastily.

'But for a start, why don't you enter the beauty contest? It's tomorrow afternoon. Think about it. You'd be sure to win.'

'I don't know,' Rona hesitated. After they'd said goodnight and later when she was taking off her make-up and getting ready for bed, she thought, Why not?

She looked in the mirror and her eyes seemed to have an extra sparkle. Well, it had been a wonderful evening I wonder if I dare, she thought. But then there was no-one here— no Father, no Aunt Lizzie, no Doug to say, 'Don't'. There was nothing to stop her.

I will enter the contest, she decided.


## AN ANNOUNCEMENT FROM AUNT LIZZIE

As the girls lined up for the parade, Rona began to have misgivings. 'I hate the thought of walking round the pool and everyone watching me,' she said. 'Why did I ever let Jake persuade me into this?'

But it was too late now, so she gave a nervous smile to where Nancy was sitting among the spectators and stole a quick glance at the other contestants.

There was one dark-haired girl in a pure white swimsuit. I could never look like that, Rona decided. Still, she thought, now that she was here she would just have to do her best.

Walk slowly, she'd been told, hold the card with your number in front of you, and smile at the judges.

So Rona stood as tall as she could and held

her card, number 12, in front of her. The girls set off, walking round the pool, and Rona remembered to smile at the judges—two men from the entertainment staff and one of the girls who had organised the event.

She smiled, feeling nothing like as carefree as she looked, and kept on smiling, until she had been right round the pool.

'There. That's over.' She had caught a glimpse of Nancy, applauding like mad, and Jake standing at the back of the crowd, giving her a thumbs-up.

'We'll be announcing the results in just a few minutes,' the announcer's voice came over the tannoy. 'And then we'll see who the lucky girl is. So just have patience, folks. Will it be your favourite? We'll just have to wait and see!'

Well, anyway, I'm glad I bought the new swimsuit, thought Rona. The other girls all looked so smart.

She was only half listening when the announcer bounded up to the microphone and called out, 'At last, folks! Here we are. In third place, number fourteen.'

A slim red-haired girl left the small group and walked towards the judges' table.

'In second place, number five. Come along—number five. And finally the winner . . . number twelve.'

'That's you!' the dark-haired girl nudged Rona. 'On you go. Congratulations!' She

130

wasn't over-sophisticated at all, thought Rona, as the girl smiled at her.

Quite bemused and convinced that the judges had made a mistake, Rona slowly made her way to the dais. The three judges shook her hand and the entertainments girl draped a sash over Rona's shoulders. There was an outburst of applause, and Rona waved shyly. She couldn't believe this was happening to her.

'Now for the photos.' At first Rona had her picture taken on her own and then with the judges. 'Your name and address please,' said the organiser. 'We'd like a picture in the local paper!'

'Oh, please,' said Rona shyly. 'I don't think . . .'

'The folk in your town will be thrilled to see Miss Nineteen Fifty-Three,' the girl assured her.

And then there seemed to be a crowd around Rona, congratulating her. Jake pushed his way through.

'Well done!' he put an arm around her. 'I knew you'd do it. And now what's the next step—becoming a professional model, maybe?'

'I haven't thought about it.' Rona was in a daze. 'It's too early—too much to take in.'

She was still wondering what Father, and Aunt Lizzie, would say when her picture appeared in *The Kirkton Advertiser*.

'We'll talk about it later,' said Jake, holding her arm in a possessive grip.

It was a glorious evening, still warm after the heat of the day. 'Too good to be indoors,' said Jake as he met Rona at the door of the dance hall. 'What about a walk down to the sea?'

Hand-in-hand they walked down towards the shore and Rona, still bemused by the events of the day, thought she had never been so happy.

'I wish this could go on and on,' she said softly.

'Me, too!' Jake looked down at her. 'You really are beautiful. The judges made the right choice.'

'It's a pity it all has to end,' she said. It was hard to imagine going back to the daily routine of the shop. 'I wish . . .'

'What do you wish, Cinderella?' he said teasingly.

'I wish I could train as a model,' Rona confessed. 'It's what I've wanted for years. But it's impossible. It costs money to go to one of these model academies, and my father . . .' she bit her lip, not wanting to admit that her father would never agree to her being a model.

'Why not?' Jake lit a cigarette and looked into the distance. 'It's not an impossible dream.'

'For me it is.'

'Nonsense,' he said briskly. 'Listen,

132

Cinderella. I know people who run these agencies. You could easily get a place. They're looking out for girls just like you—slim, graceful, who know how to dress, how to walk. And the fact that you've been crowned a holiday camp princess means you're halfway there,' he added with a smile.

'But I don't—I mean I don't know how to go about applying.'

'Leave it all to me. I told you about what I can do, didn't I—I'm in the entertainment business. I've got contacts and I could pull strings for you.'

'Would you?' Rona's eyes lit up.

'For you,' he took her hand. 'Anything. Just you leave it all to me. It may take a week or two,' he said, 'but I'll be in touch. Don't forget to give me your address before we say goodbye. That sounds very final, doesn't it, but I promise you, I'll be in touch very soon.'

'Can I write to you?' said Rona.

'Better not, sweetheart. I'm all over the country, never quite know when I'll be at home. But trust me, I'll ring all the agencies I know. They're crying out for girls just like you.'

*         *         *

Rona went back to the chalet with her head full of plans and dreams and it seemed as if her heart was singing. It wasn't just his parting words—'You do realise, don't you, that you

133

are very special to me,' and the way he looked at her, and his lingering kiss.

She suddenly felt that this week a whole new world had opened up before her. Soon, she would be on her way. First Edinburgh, then who knows, London. She would no longer be Rona Maclaren, the baker's daughter, but someone whose photo was in newspapers and magazines. 'I could change your life,' he had whispered to her as they said goodnight. Rona looked up at him and he smiled down at her. This evening, she knew, was just the beginning of something wonderful.

\*     \*     \*

'Well that's one good thing,' said Rona, as she read the piece in *The Advertiser*, the local paper.

'What's that?' asked Nancy.

'They don't publish photos—well, only if it's something like a big wedding or the visit of royalty, or something very important.'

'But they've printed a report about you being the holiday princess,' said Nancy, leaning over her friend's shoulder.

'Only a small paragraph,' said Rona. 'And not many people will read it,' she added hopefully.

But she was wrong. Customers kept coming into the shop to congratulate her.

'My, you've done well,' said one. 'A pity

there wasn't a photo of you.'

Angus had said very little, except, 'Ah well, what's done is done. I should never have let you go away with that Nancy.'

Nancy's father said much the same. 'I thought that girl would have had more sense, or I wouldn't have let you go on holiday with her.'

But generally, the two fathers, meeting in the street agreed. A bathing beauty contest—well, it hadn't been a local contest, and no harm had been done.

'She's a bonnie lass, your Rona,' said Nancy's father, and Angus felt quite proud. Rona was turning out well, after all. He sighed as he thought of his Ruby, and how he'd tried to bring up his daughter as she would have wanted.

Aunt Lizzie simply sniffed as she read the report in the local paper, and said nothing. She was strange these days, thought Rona, as if her presence was here in the shop and at home, but she was somehow far away.

As for Callum, he didn't know whether to be pleased or not. They met occasionally now, but somehow the closeness of their friendship had gone.

Rona didn't know whether she cared or not. She liked Callum, but he had never made her feel the way Jake did.

'I'd quite have liked to see you winning the contest,' Callum said, 'but I don't know if I'd have wanted my girl parading in front of all these people!'

'Callum!' Rona was becoming really cross by now.

She turned to Callum. 'This is nineteen fifty-three, and anyway, it's none of your business what I do.'

'It is.' His face flushed. 'You're my girl after all.'

'Indeed I am not,' Rona said angrily.

'Well, I thought,' he mumbled, 'I thought we were going steady.'

'I can't think what gave you that idea,' she said loftily, quite forgetting that only a few months ago she had wished for more than just friendship between them.

'Anyway,' she added, 'we're only friends. In fact,' she said a little breathlessly, 'I've actually met someone.'

'That was quick,' he said, looking a little surprised. 'Just a holiday romance, that's all it'll be.'

'You're quite wrong,' Rona was emphatic. 'It's more than that. And he's going to help me get into a model agency. He says I've a great future ahead as a model.'

'For goodness' sake!' Callum burst out laughing. 'It's turned your head, you winning this competition.'

Rona was incensed. 'You don't know anything about anything,' she burst out. 'Living here, never going anywhere. You don't know what I could do. He says I could easily get a job in London.'

'Forget it.' Callum was calmer now. 'Oh, you did well, winning the competition, but it was just a bit of fun. It'll never lead to anything. Now, what do you want to do this evening? The pictures, dancing?'

Rona spoke very slowly. 'I don't want to go out with you again, Callum—is that perfectly clear? You and I have nothing in common, and I won't be sneered at like that.'

'If that's the way of it.' To Rona's surprise, he turned and walked away without a backward glance.

'Well!' she thought. 'I'm well rid of him.' But she thought perversely that he might have tried to make her change her mind. She watched him as he crossed the road and strode along the High Street. She had more to think of, she told herself. She had a whole new future to plan.

\*        \*        \*

It was a particularly busy time in the baker's. Families on holiday in the caravans came in to buy pies and bread; holidaymakers wanted boxes of shortbread to take home as presents.

After the success of the Coronation window, Angus was persuaded by Rona to let her decorate a holiday display with buckets and spades and shrimping nets borrowed from the

137

toy shop, surrounding pies and sausage rolls and picnic fare.

Although she was busy and preoccupied with work in the shop, Rona still felt a little uneasy about Aunt Lizzie. She was, well, somewhat jumpy—she rose quickly from the table whenever the phone rang, and greeted the postman at the door. Rona too was a little edgy.

She had still not heard from Jake, though she knew that he wouldn't forget his promise of introductions to the model agencies. Surely, she thought, he would write soon.

Doug said he had noticed nothing out of the way about Aunt Lizzie and Angus was far too busy in the shop. The new assistant, Elsie, was turning out well. She had boundless energy, and was becoming known to many of the customers.

She and Rona worked well together. It was good, Rona thought, to have someone of her own age to laugh with, and share a joke about some of the more demanding customers.

But still, she worried about Aunt Lizzie.

Things came to a head one late summer afternoon. The shop was closed for the half-day and Angus had strolled along to the bowling green.

Doug was out with his friends, Rona was sifting in the garden in the sun, a magazine on her lap, dreamily reliving that wonderful week and remembering how Jake had looked at her, and trying to recall the sound of his voice.

Aunt Lizzie was in her room—she spent a lot of time there, writing letters. After a little while, she came down the stairs, dressed to go out in her summer coat and her hat .

She had a letter in her hand. 'I'm just away to the post box,' she called to Rona. 'To get the lifting.'

Rona nodded, wondering vaguely why it was important.

But Aunt Lizzie was back before long. 'There, that's it done!' she said as she vanished into the house.

Rona was puzzled, but she didn't ask any questions. After a bit, she rose and put the magazine aside and went to help Aunt Lizzie with the tea.

'We'll just have cold ham and a bit of salad. Away you go and pick a lettuce,' she told Rona. Angus's hard work in the garden had paid off. There was a row of crisp Webb's Wonder lettuces, and Rona pulled some radishes to go with the salad.

\*       \*       \*

'A grand tea,' said Angus, spreading a piece of bread with butter, and passing over his cup for a refill. 'You do us proud, Lizzie.'

Aunt Lizzie flushed, and laid down her knife and fork. 'If you've all finished, I've something to tell you.'

139

Doug stopped eating, surprised. Rona gazed at Aunt Lizzie, who fiddled with the Cairngorm brooch at the neck of her pale blue silk blouse.

'You might as well know now,' she said.

'So what is it, Lizzie?' asked Angus. 'What have you got to tell us?'

'I'm leaving you—leaving Kirkton,' said Aunt Lizzie, all in a rush.

'Is that so?' Angus stared at her. 'And what's brought this about? Where are you going?'

'I'm going to Glencraig,' said Aunt Lizzie, her voice trembling a little.

'But why?' Rona found her voice. 'Maisie's fine again, isn't she? Why do you want to go?'

'After all these years—it's a bit sudden, isn't it?' said Angus. 'So what's made you want to upstakes and leave us? Why?'

Aunt Lizzie drew a deep breath and said, looking round the table at them all, 'Because I've met someone and I'm going to marry him, that's why.'


## 'I HAVEN'T HEARD FROM JAKE'

'Cripes!' Doug gave a low whistle while looking shocked. Angus seemed at a complete loss.

'Well,' he said slowly. 'I must say this is a

140

surprise, Lizzie I'd no idea there was anything in the offing. So who's the lucky man?' he added trying to be jocular.

'I don't know why you should all be so taken aback,' said Lizzie with a touch of her old manner.

'Go on, tell us.' Rona had been silent for a moment or two. But now, she said, 'Who is it? Where did you meet him? Tell us all about him.'

Aunt Lizzie looked round them all. 'He's a widower. I met him at Maisie's—she's got a neighbour who's been a great help, and Malcolm's her brother. He calls in and does the odd job like clearing the gutters. We got chatting and well, he asked me to go for a walk. I did a bit to help him in his house,' she said, ' Oh, that house of his, poor soul, he's not done much since his wife passed on. Anyway, we've been writing to each other since I came back.'

So that was why she was watching for postie every day, thought Rona with a smile.

'And,' Aunt Lizzie finished, 'he's asked me to marry him. He's got a house in the village, a good size, and there's some beautiful furniture,' she added. 'Oh, I think we'll get along fine.'

Fancy, thought Rona, suppressing a smile, getting married for good furniture. It's not at all romantic. But then she felt very mean. Why shouldn't Aunt Lizzie take a pride in having her own home with nice furniture?

It wasn't kind to smile at Aunt Lizzie's romance. Not that it was romantic—but none the worse for that.

Aunt Lizzie would make a good, caring wife, and if she was bossy and very particular, well, perhaps he'd enjoy being looked after.

'So,' said Angus, 'when are we going to meet your intended?' Rona could almost have said that Aunt Lizzie blushed.

'He's coming down for the day next Saturday—I've asked him to come for tea. And we're to discuss the arrangements then.'

'Are you to be married from here?' Rona's thoughts raced ahead.

'I doubt it,' said Aunt Lizzie briskly. 'Just a small quiet ceremony up in Glencraig. It wouldn't be fitting, a big wedding—not at our age.'

'You've not even told us anything about him,' said Angus, 'such as his name, and what he does.'

'He's called Malcolm—Malcolm Watt, and he had a plumbing business. Of course, he's retired, and has been some years.'

'Well, I'll look forward to meeting Mr Watt —Malcolm,' said Angus kindly. 'And I'm sure we hope you'll be very happy. Isn't that right?' He turned to Doug and Rona.

'The only thing,' Aunt Lizzie said, not acknowledging his good wishes, 'is that I'm kind of worried about leaving you folks to cope

142

on your own.'

'Think nothing of it,' said Angus. 'You've done us proud all these years, and the bairns are grown now. You deserve a bit life of your own. Anyway,' he continued, 'Rona did fine when you were away looking after Maisie. She can make a grand pot of soup—near as good as yours, Lizzie,' he said with a smile.

'Aye,' Lizzie agreed, 'and you're doing all right in the shop, especially now you've got Elsie.'

Rona felt as if someone had poured a bucket of cold water over her.

What about me? she raged inwardly. Am I to be a housekeeper just like Aunt Lizzie? Don't I deserve a bit of happiness, something to look forward to? She thought of Jake and his promises.

Suppose he got her an interview, and he'd said it was certain he would, suppose she had a chance to train as a model, and had to give it up because she was needed at home, and was needed to make soup and mince as good as Aunt Lizzie's.

Suddenly she felt that her first pleasure at hearing Aunt Lizzie's news had gone.

Oh, it was all very well for Aunt Lizzie and her widower who needed looking after and it was all very well for Father who had a daughter at home who would fill the gap left by Aunt Lizzie's departure. And it was all very well for Doug, who didn't care about anything

143

much except cars and motorbikes and sitting down to a good meal.

Rona felt as if her chances of romance were vanishing into thin air, and she could see nothing much ahead of her but years of a dull, monotonous life.

Still, she smiled at Aunt Lizzie. 'I'm really pleased for you,' she said, as she felt a lump in her throat.

\*     \*     \*

The weeks went by. There was no word from Jake and Callum, too, seemed to be keeping a distance.

'I haven't heard from Jake, and he promised to write,' Rona confessed to Nancy. 'He said . . .' she hesitated, 'that he would be in touch. He has lots of contact with modelling agencies, and he thought he could easily get me an interview.'

Nancy looked doubtful. 'What does he do? How does he know these people?'

'He's in the entertainment business.' Rona was a little defensive.

Nancy hesitated. She hated to disillusion her friend, but wasn't it better to tell her now?

'Wait a bit,' she advised. 'I'm sure he'll be in touch with you.'

But there was no word from Jake. The holiday was beginning to seem a distant dream.

144

Although two girls from West Fife that they'd met while on holiday—Bet and Isla—had written, and Bet sent copies of a photo they'd taken of Rona and Nancy, standing in front of their chalet.

'Bet says they're hoping to come to Kirkton to visit a cousin and maybe we could meet up,' said Nancy, reading the letter.

'That would be fun.' Rona had liked the two lively girls when they'd shared a table in the huge dining hall, and laughed at their stories of life in the linen factory where they both worked.

It would be good, thought Rona, to have something to laugh about. She was still anxious about the future—what would happen when Aunt Lizzie left?

By now the family had met Malcolm. He was a solid, good-natured man in his sixties, who'd taken Rona's hand in a huge grasp and said, 'So you're the niece. My, your auntie's told me all about you—nothing but good,' he'd added hurriedly. 'A fine wee housekeeper, and a real ray of sunshine about the house.'

Rona was quite sure this wasn't true. She could hardly credit Aunt Lizzie with such a flowery phrase, but it was kind and well-meaning of the good-natured Mr Watt (or Uncle Malcolm, as he'd asked them to call him).

So it was pleasant to have a half-day meeting up with Bet and Isla off the Kirkcaldy bus, and spending the afternoon touring the shops.

'Not that I've a lot to spend after the holiday,' said Isla, 'but it's great to see different shops from home.' They spent an hour at least, trying on clothes, deciding on a new shade of lipstick, choosing a wooden toy for a small nephew.

Although it was a half-day, they insisted on going to see Maclaren's. 'My word,' said Bet in admiration, 'did you do the window yourself?' They gazed at Rona's display of the shrimping nets and buckets and spades. 'Are you not the clever one? I couldn't have thought of that not if you'd paid me a fortune,' said Isla.

Finally, they sat over ice-creams and coffee in the Cosy Café. Rona remembered with a slight pang how Callum had brought her here and they'd watched the flickering pictures on the television set and how he'd chosen her favourite tunes from the jukebox. A boy and girl affair, she thought. That was over anyway.

'That was a real good holiday,' said Isla, sipping her coffee.

'A lot of laughs,' Nancy agreed.

'And quite a few holiday romances,' added Bet. 'Even though they don't last,' she said realistically.

'Remember that one, what was his name? Jake. The airline pilot?' said Bet.

Rona felt suddenly apprehensive. 'Jake?'

146

'You know, medium height, dark curly hair, very smooth talker.' Bet laughed.

'I thought you and he maybe,' her voice tailed off as she saw Rona's face.

'Ooops, have I put my foot in it?'

'No, not at all,' said Rona hastily. 'Yes, I did meet him but,' she hesitated, 'I didn't know he was an airline pilot. I thought he was in entertainment.'

'Is that what he told you?' Bet shook her head. 'What a fibber. He told me I'd have a great future as an air hostess. Me? Imagine! I've never been in a plane and nothing on earth would get me up in the air.' She roared with laughter.

Rona was silent for a few moments and the others looked at her. 'Has he, I mean, has he written to you?' she asked Bet.

Bet shook her head. 'No, he hasn't and I wouldn't expect him to. Ships that pass in the night and all that. Never mind, it was fun while it lasted and he was a really nifty dancer. What about you? Has he written?'

'No, he hasn't. And I wouldn't really have expected him to.' Nancy was about to say something and then thought better of it.

As they waved the two girls off on the bus, she turned to Rona, 'You'd best forget him and his promises.'

'I've been a bit of a fool,' said Rona bitterly.

Nancy laid a hand on her friend's arm. 'Don't worry, he's not worth another thought.

147

There's as good fish in the sea,' she said, and as she spoke, she thought this was not much comfort to poor Rona.

Well, that's that, thought Rona as she made her way home. An end to my dreams of being a model. Let's face it, she told herself firmly, I'm not cut out to be a model. You need poise and personality and I'm just an ordinary girl, maybe with a decent figure, but that's all. I'd never make a real model.

She thought, sadly about how foolish she'd been believing his stories and promises. She realised now that Jake had never really talked about himself.

And what if he had exaggerated, made all kinds of promises he wasn't able to keep? It was her own fault, Rona decided, aware that the moonlight and the romantic atmosphere often made things more exciting than they really were.

A pity, she thought briefly, that she had to fall for someone like Jake, when she'd met so many ordinary, but very pleasant young men during the week—young men who'd been eager to get to know her. Romance, she thought, wasn't always what it seemed.

She pushed open the garden gate. 'I'd better settle for being a ray of sunshine around the house.' And she went indoors to peel the potatoes and shell the peas and set the table for tea.

# A SURPRISE FROM DOUG

It was astonishing how quickly things happened. One moment Aunt Lizzie was housekeeper to the Maclaren family, cashier in the shop and a familiar figure round the streets of Kirkton.

The next, it seemed, she had gone and was settled in Glenmuir, the wife of a retired businessman. And she appeared to be very contented in her new role. There were letters weekly, detailing her busy life—she and Malcolm had joined the indoor bowling club, she had been welcomed at the Guild, and there were frequent outings.

Malcolm had taken her in his new Austin Cambridge up to Pitlochry for a sight of the autumn colours: they had driven up north and had spent a few days in Banchory.

She was kept busy in her new home, cooking, looking after Malcolm, and taking a pride in cleaning and polishing. She would ask how they were getting on—was Rona remembering that Angus liked porridge done a certain way, and the best kind of starch to use on the tablecloths?

Rona ignored this advice—her father never complained about the porridge. By now she had mastered the skill of making it without lumps. And as for starching tablecloths . . . .'

Does she think I have nothing else to do?' muttered Rona to herself. She had never starched a tablecloth in her life and wasn't going to begin now.

*And be sure*, added Aunt Lizzie, *you dust the tops of your doors.*

Rona gritted her teeth and was glad that Aunt Lizzie was 50 odd miles away. Still, she managed the housekeeping—it was a busy time in the shop and between home and work, Rona had little time for regrets about Jake and longing for someone of her own.

Doug seemed preoccupied these days and, to Rona's surprise, he began to take much more interest in his appearance.

'You'd not believe it,' she told Nancy, 'he's really fussy about shining his shoes, and he's started using brilliantine on his hair!'

'It's a girl,' said Nancy knowingly. 'These are all the signs.'

She had two elder brothers of her own, so was wise about these things. 'You wait—he's met someone.'

'He hasn't said anything,' said Rona, remembering the disastrous relationship with Neela.

'He'll be bringing her home one of these days,' Nancy prophesied.

Rona looked doubtful. 'Well, we'll have to wait and see.' They didn't have to wait long.

One evening, Doug, looking embarrassed and said, 'Can you make your steak and kidney pie for the tea on Sunday.'

Rona looked surprised. 'Yes, if you like.'

'With plenty of gravy,' Doug added.

'Hey, what's all this?' Rona stopped wiping the sink in a rather perfunctory way. 'I often make a steak pie on a Sunday.'

'Yes, well . . .' Doug paused then said all in a rush, 'and maybe a trifle.'

'If you like.' Rona was puzzled. 'Why? It's not a birthday.'

'Well, it's a bit special.'

'All right.' Rona had planned to go with Nancy to the pictures to see *Roman Holiday*. She'd heard that Audrey Hepburn was wonderful and as for Gregory Peck . . . but Doug didn't often ask her for a favour—he ate up everything that was before him and often had second helpings.

'Is there,' she hesitated, 'is there a special reason?'

'I'm wanting to bring someone for her tea!'

'A girl?'

'That's not what I said.'

'You said "for her tea". This kind of argument was common between the brother and sister.

'Well, it is a girl,' said Doug. 'And I want her to get a good impression.'

Rona didn't know what to say. He had only once brought a girl home, and that was a painfully shy, tongue-tied creature, who said only, 'Thanks,' or I don't mind' and gazed at

151

Doug throughout the meal with an expression of adoration that annoyed Rona intensely. She hadn't lasted long, that one.

But what about the girls he met at the dancing? Large, energetic girls who didn't mind Doug birling them round and round, rosy-faced outdoor girls who laughed a great deal. It would be one of these girls, Rona decided.

'So,' she asked hesitantly, 'what's her name? And what's she like?'

'She's Austrian,' said Doug, as if the information was dragged out of him. 'Her name's Erika.'

'And where did you meet her? What's she doing here?'

'You ask a lot of questions.' Doug refused to satisfy Rona's curiosity. 'You'll meet her on Saturday.'

\* \* \*

'How interesting,' said Nancy. 'Where do you think he met her?'

'He's not saying. I wonder if it's serious, him bringing her to tea?'

Rona was determined to make a special effort for Doug and his new girlfriend, so she starched the tablecloth and cleaned the silver.

She hummed to herself as she made the pastry for the steak pie. What would the Austrian girl be like, she wondered. Tall, slim and blonde, probably.

As she put the finishing touches to the table that Sunday, and decorated the trifle with cherries and small silver balls, she looked approvingly at what she had done.

'My, this is a grand spread,' said Angus. 'You've fair done us proud.'

Rona had hardly had time to think of her own appearance, but she tidied her hair, and changed into her tweed skirt and a new pale pink sweater that Aunt Lizzie had knitted for her.

'They're here!' She hurried to open the door with a wide welcoming smile.

The girl shook hands formally, and Rona had to stop herself looking astonished.

For this wasn't the young girl she'd imagined but a much older woman—she must be at least thirty, thought Rona.

Doug was clearly very proud of Erika. He helped her off with her coat in a way that made Rona smile to herself—Doug being gallant, this was something new.

Erika's speech was hesitant and Rona quickly realised that her guest spoke very little English.

'Thank you,' said Erika. 'It is kind of you. To ask me.'

'Not at all,' Rona tried to recover herself. 'We are glad to meet you.'

Where she wondered, had Doug met Erika? They seemed such a strange pairing and yet

Doug was clearly besotted and could hardly keep his eyes off Erika.

She was pleasant and wholesome, Rona thought—a clear, fresh complexion and her fair hair done in braids that were looped around her head. She wore a simple dark blue suit and a spotless white blouse edged with lace, and no make-up at all. Quite different from all Doug's previous girlfriends.

This, thought Rona was going to be a little difficult. She had not expected that Doug's new girlfriend would speak so little English. So she tried to make up for the long silences by smiling and talking about Kirkton and Fife— she knew very little about Austria, though she remembered school geography lessons about the mountains and the river Danube, was it? But she could hardly keep the conversation going all afternoon by talking about the rivers of Austria.

Father was a kindly and good-natured host, though he, too, was fairly silent. And as for Doug, he simply gazed at Erika with admiration.

'Please sit down at the table.' Rona gestured.

'Can I help?' Doug leapt up. Rona stared at him. This was the first time he had ever offered.

'No, thanks,' she said brusquely and carried in the steak and kidney pie, piping hot and with a wonderful and promising aroma.

'My, this is a grand change,' said Angus. 'It's usually pies or bridies for a Sunday tea.'

'You're doing us proud today, Rona,' said Doug.

'As if you usually starved,' she said more sharply than she meant, as she handed round the potatoes and carrots.

Erika had a good appetite and praised everything. 'It's good,' she said, smiling broadly and Rona warmed to her.

She wondered, though, as she dished up the trifle, how they would get through the evening. There was very little to talk about and yet she was longing to ask questions—where did Doug meet her? How had she come to Kirkton? Where did she work? How old was she?

After tea, Doug said, 'We'll do the dishes.'

Rona was so taken aback that she didn't protest, but allowed Doug to roll up his sleeves and begin washing up, while Erika picked up a dish towel. As she cleared the table she could hear a low murmur of conversation—or at least she could hear Doug's voice and an occasional word from Erika.

Afterwards as Angus settled into his armchair with the *Sunday Post*, Doug put a few records on the radiogram.

But even so, it was a long evening as Rona tried to be polite to this smiling, silent girl.

Finally she produced tea and shortbread. Angus yawned, got up and said, 'I'm away to my bed.' He shook hands with Erika,

155

said, 'Good to meet you,' and made his way upstairs.

'I'll see you home, Erika,' said Doug at last and helped her with her coat.

'I have enjoyed it,' she said very slowly and carefully.

'You must come again soon,' Rona returned politely.

'I do not speak much English,' she said, 'but Doug, he teaches me.'

Doug smiled fondly at her. 'You'll soon learn,' he said.

After they'd gone, Rona tidied the kitchen finding that the cups and plates were all in the wrong place—that was the trouble, she thought, when you let someone else into your kitchen, but her mind was buzzing with questions. Where had Doug met her? Where had she come from? She was determined to ask him when he returned.

'I'll lock up, will I?' She heard Doug come in, and he put his head round the kitchen door. 'Grand meal that—thanks.'

'She doesn't say much, does she?' said Rona.

'Well,' Doug was defensive, 'she doesn't speak much English—yet. But she likes you.'

'Thanks for that.' Rona was tired and inclined to be snappy. 'She's a bit of a surprise, I must say, after your other girls. Where did you meet her? Where's she from? What happened to her relatives? Where is she

156

working?'

'Don't want to know much, do you? I met her on the ferry—she's working in the laundry, she's from Vienna and her parents are dead. That answer your questions?'

'Well, I suppose so.'

'And one more thing,' said Doug. 'I know she's older than me, but I'm serious about her, and she feels the same about me. So you'd better get used to the idea. This is the real thing, this time. See you in the morning.'


## A MEETING WITH CALLUM

'I just feel as if the world had been turned upside down,' said Rona. Usually, she didn't mind February and was happy to put on Wellingtons and splash through the slush to work, but this year everything seemed to have happened so quickly, first with Aunt Lizzie's departure and now Doug.

'What's she like?' Nancy was curious.

'Pleasant, quiet—hard to get to know, I'd say.'

'Doug seems to have got to know her fast enough,' Nancy smiled.

'They met on the ferry from Dundee to Tayport,' said Rona. 'Doug had been over to look at a car. He helped her with her luggage, I gather. And that was that.'

'How romantic,' sighed Nancy.

'I wish something like that would happen to me,' said Rona. She added, 'I haven't been able to find out any more. You know Doug—he'd make a clam seem almost chatty. But I understand she'd been helping a relative in Dundee and now she's working in the laundry and looking after an old lady. I must say,' Rona went on, 'she seems a hard worker. But what her background is, don't ask me, I've no idea. And I don't think Doug has either. But it doesn't seem to matter to him.'

'She won't be a gold digger then,' said Nancy.

'Not if she's after our Doug,' Rona laughed. 'He never seems to have two pennies to scrape together.'

Rona sighed. There was romance everywhere—except in her own life. Even Nancy shyly mentioned the young man she'd met at the badminton club who'd asked her to the firm's dance at Christmas.

'I'd like to get to know Erika,' Rona told Nancy. 'But somehow I don't think I will. She speaks so little English, we can never have a conversation.'

But she spoke too soon.

That February was cold and miserable and Rona was a little worried about her father. He worked so hard, up it seemed in the middle of the night to light the ovens, baking the bread—a short pause for breakfast then out on the road with the deliveries. It was a long day and he looked rather tired.

'Are you all right?' she asked one evening.

'Me? Aye, I'm fine. Don't fuss, girl,' he said abruptly. Rona didn't ask any more, but she decided to keep an eye on him.

One day he came home, and though she had prepared a tasty stew with carrots and onions, just as he liked it, he seemed to have little appetite and pushed his plate away.

'It's a grand stew, lass,' he said, 'but I'm not very hungry.' A little later, he said, 'I'm away to my bed.'

When Rona went up an hour or so afterwards, she found him tossing and turning. She brought him a hot drink of honey and lemon and laid a hand on his forehead. 'You're all hot, Father,' she said. 'I hope it's not this flu that's doing the rounds.' She looked anxious. 'You'll stay where you are. I'll bring you a hot water bottle. And never mind about the shop. I can manage.'

'No, no!' He tried to sit up.

'I've seen you baking the bread often enough,' she said firmly. 'I'll away and set my alarm.'

When she rose in the cold, dark early hours, Angus was asleep. She tapped on Doug's door and told him to look in on their father. 'I'll get the doctor if he's no better,' she said.

Doug struggled awake. 'I'll see to the deliveries,' he said. 'They'll give me time off at

159

the garage.'

'Thanks,' Rona said gratefully. 'We'll manage somehow.' That first morning was hard—although she had told Angus she knew what needed to be done, Rona found the work heavy, handling the large trays, pushing them into the oven.

When Elsie arrived at eight, Rona was already exhausted. 'Make us a cup of tea, there's a good girl,' she said. 'And then we'll get started.'

It seemed a long day. Rona ran home at dinner time and found her father still feverish and coughing. She called in at the doctor's surgery and asked him to visit, and left a key with a kindly neighbour. She tried to persuade Angus to take a little broth, but he managed only a few spoonfuls.

Then she hurried back to the shop. How on earth were they going to manage, she wondered.

That evening, Rona fell asleep by the fire and woke with a start. This wouldn't do—she had to be up in the middle of the night to light the ovens and begin the day's work. By now Angus was asleep.

'It's this flu,' the doctor had reassured her earlier in the evening. 'Keep him warm and give him lots of liquids. And don't let him go back to work till he's completely better.'

'Easier said than done,' Rona answered. But she was determined to manage the bakery as well as she could while Angus was ill. Though Doug was helpful—he did the deliveries, and at home, washed up, set the fires and carried out the ashes.

But the early rise the next morning was a real struggle. As she washed hurriedly and put on her warmest clothes, she wondered how long they could keep going. The weather was bitterly cold too—she remembered the old saying, *As the day lengthens, the cold strengthens.*

She had lit the ovens and was kneading the dough for the loaves when she heard a sound, like a sort of tapping. Someone at the shop door? It couldn't possibly be—not at this time of the morning. She went on pounding the dough.

There it was again. She wiped her hands, and went to look out the glass-fronted door of the shop. To her astonishment, a face looked in at her.

'What are you doing here?' she said, astonished.

'Please—I come to help.'

Rona opened the door, and there wrapped in a thick woollen coat with a scarf around her head, was Erika.

'Why did you come?'

'I come to help,' said Erika simply 'Doug told me about your father.' She made her way through to the back of the shop to the bakehouse.

161

Rona didn't know what to say. It was good of Erika, but she wondered, could she really be of help?

Erika seemed to know what she was thinking. 'I know about baking bread,' she said. 'In Vienna, my father has, had, a *konditorei*. You say pastry-cook. He make loaves too, fancy loaves.' As she was talking, she took off her coat—she was wearing a large apron and she rolled up her sleeves. 'Now you make the dough?'

All through the early morning, Erika worked, saying little, but seeming to know exactly what was wanted. When Elsie arrived at eight as usual, she put on her coat and wound the scarf round her head 'I go now—to laundry. I come back tomorrow—is OK?'

'Is very much OK,' said Rona who didn't know how she could have managed.

'She's been really wonderful,' she told Doug later.

'I told you she was a wonder,' said Doug—and he beamed with pride.

*　　　*　　　*

Gradually Angus regained his strength, though Rona insisted that he didn't come back to the shop until he was completely recovered.

At least now, she didn't feel so desperately alone. There was Doug, helping out with the deliveries, and Elsie working hard in the shop, and Erika—a tower of strength, whether she was turning out a batch of brown loaves, or rolling the pastry for sausage rolls and bridies.

What about her parents, Rona wondered. Erika had mentioned her father had been a pastry-cook, but what had happened to her mother, and were there any brothers and sisters?

She was getting to know Erika better, but it was early days and she didn't feel that she could pry. Even though Erika's English was improving every day, it was still difficult to have a long conversation.

Now Angus was regaining his appetite and Rona took pleasure in making dishes that he would enjoy.

'I've a nice piece of haddock for tonight, Father,' she said.

'Not steamed in milk, I hope,' said Angus with a twinkle in his eye. 'I've had enough sick folks' fare to last me for many a day.'

'Is that so?' Rona tried to look stern. 'And how would you like it done?'

'Fried in breadcrumbs,' said Angus. 'And maybe with chips?'

'Now I know you're recovering.' Rona was pleased to see that he looked more like his old self.

After tea, Angus sat down in his favourite chair by the fire and picked-up the local paper. He started at the back, as he usually did, scanning the adverts.

'Well now, this is a bit of news.'

'What's that?' Rona sat down opposite him with her mending basket.

'Harefield Farm—up for sale next week by public roup,' he said. 'There's five-hundred acres and two cottar houses—I reckon they'll get a good price. Is that not the farm that belongs to young Callum's family?'

'Yes,' said Rona coolly. 'It could well be.'

Angus looked sharply across at her. It was some time since young Callum had called at the house—had he and Rona fallen out, he wondered. A pity, if so. He'd liked the lad with his fresh, open face and hearty laugh.

Rona could almost feel her heart thudding. Why was Callum's father selling up? And what would that mean for Callum?

But it doesn't matter to me, she told herself. Ever since they'd had that disagreement— when she had won the beauty competition— they had been like strangers. Sometimes she met him in the town and he'd wave or say, 'hello', but that was all. And once she had seen him talking to a fair-haired girl at the bus stop, talking and laughing as if they were very good friends.

Not that it mattered, not in the slightest. He'd been unreasonable, though she admitted she had flown off the handle. And anyway, no-one was going to tell her what to do.

It was perhaps a few weeks later on a blustery March day which sent the wind sighing through the trees, and people trying to stand upright as they stumbled, heads bowed against the wind, along the street.

Rona had left the shop for a short time to go to the butcher's and the greengrocer's and was making her way along the High Street, her scarf wound round her neck and her head bent against the high wind that whistled round the corner. Suddenly she bumped into someone. 'I'm so sorry,' she said, as she regained her balance.

'Hey, there!' Two strong arms went round her, as she heard a familiar voice.

'Oh, Callum! I'm sorry,' she said again.

He smiled down at her. 'You look laden— can I help carry some of your shopping? It's a wild sort of day.'

Rona hesitated. 'Thank you,' she said. 'I can manage.'

'Well, I'll walk along with you. How's Mr Maclaren?' he asked. 'I heard he'd been under the weather.'

'He's better,' said Rona. There was a long pause then she said, 'I saw in the paper, your father's farm's for sale.'

'Yes?' Callum nodded. 'It's coming up at the roup next week.'

'And what does that mean?' Rona didn't like to sound curious.

'You mean why are they selling? Oh, it all got a bit too much for my father—he's not getting any younger. So Tom will take over the

165

other farm, Langton—and Sandy's got a job in a firm, Mackie's—that sells farm machinery. Just the job for him. He never was very keen on the farm. And my parents are moving to a bungalow in the town.' He grinned. 'So it's all working out well.'

'And—' Rona hardly dared ask, 'what will you do?'

'I've been thinking for a long time. I'm quite interested in going to Canada. I've been over to Dundee to the travel agent there, just to make enquiries. There's the ship, the *Captain Cook*, sailing in a couple of months' time.'

'Where to?' Rona could hardly get the words out.

'Glasgow to Montreal.'

'Have you a job to go to?'

'I've a cousin not far from Montreal—he wants me to go in with him—they've a store, selling all kinds of goods.'

'So you've got plans,' Rona said, not looking at him.

'Well,' he said thoughtfully, 'there's nothing definite as yet. But there's not much to keep me here.' Then suddenly, he said, 'Rona, I know it's not the time and place, but would you meet me later? I'd like to talk to you.'

'I suppose so.'

He handed over her bags and pushed open the shop door. 'See you tonight, then,' he said and she watched him stride off with that long, loping walk that had been so familiar.

As she filled up a tray of potato scones, Rona's mind was not on her work. Her thoughts whirled round. Somehow she had always imagined Callum there in Kirkton, but if he went away, would she miss him? Or would she find someone else—maybe a new romance?

She wasn't at all sure of her feelings, but one thing was certain, she would have to get used to life without Callum nearby. He would go to Canada, enter his cousin's business, meet a nice girl, marry and raise a family. Some time, in the far future, they would all come back on holiday to see his family.

She imagined meeting him in the street—a little older, of course, but with the same smile and a trace of Canadian accent.

Maybe she would be married too, and they'd exchange in a friendly way, news of their families.

'Rona, what about the order for Seaview? They've just rung.'

Rona pushed all thoughts of Callum and the future to the back of her mind. 'Sorry' she said. 'I'd almost forgotten.' That wouldn't do, she told herself. Keep your mind on the job, she decided.

That evening she wondered what she should wear, but there was really no decision to make. It was still cold, a strong wind howling through the trees, so it was her thick brown woollen coat and a woolly hat, or nothing.

167

'Sorry to bring you out on such a miserable night,' said Callum when he arrived.

'Time for a cup of coffee?'

They sat opposite each other in the café as they had done so often. In the background someone had put coins into the jukebox and the sound of loud music made conversation difficult.

Rona sipped her coffee and unwrapped the paper from a chocolate biscuit. Callum grimaced. 'It's not much of a place,' he said, as the door opened and a group of teenagers burst in, chattering and bringing with them a blast of cold air.

They crowded round the jukebox and someone asked, 'Can we not have the television on?'

'That's enough,' said Callum firmly. 'Have you finished your coffee? Then let's go.'

He took her arm as they left the café. 'What about walking along the front?' he suggested.

Rona shivered slightly.

'Come on,' he said with a grin. 'It'll be bracing.'

In a little while Rona found she was enjoying the wind bringing colour into her cheeks, and the sight of the waves dashing against the promenade wall.

'We'll be out of the wind here,' said Callum as he drew her into a wooden shelter along the promenade. 'And not likely to get blown away.'

168

He put his arm around her and they sat silently for a bit. 'We're the only pebbles on the beach,' said Callum into the silence.

Rona turned and looked up at him—he was so familiar to her, the sound of his voice and the comfort of his arms. Suddenly she couldn't imagine what life would be like without him.

'Rona,' he said, hesitating, 'I know you probably don't feel the same about me and I'm not one for making pretty speeches, but I love you, and I always will. I wonder—would you come to Canada with me? Marry me, I mean?' He stopped. 'I'm not putting this very well, but you get the message?' He paused.

'Oh, Callum,' said Rona and she felt as if a load had been lifted from her shoulders. All these months that had seemed so drab and so lacking in any promise—and here was a whole new future opening up for her. A future, with Callum.

'I think,' he said slowly, 'you feel the same way about me. Although we had our differences?' He went on quickly, 'And we probably will in future, disagree, I mean. I've a quick temper.'

'Me, too,' Rona put in.

'Then we're meant for each other,' said Callum. 'We'd get on well together. I know I could make you happy, Rona. Say you will.'

Rona hesitated. On the one hand, she desperately wanted him. But on the other . . .

'I wish!' she said slowly. 'Oh Callum, it's not

that I don't love you. I've been so lonely and miserable without you.'

'Well, then?' He looked puzzled. 'What's the matter?'

'Don't you see,' she said, 'I'm needed here. Who would help in the shop, and who would look after Father and Doug and the home? I can't just leave them and go off to Canada.'

'You need to have a life of your own,' Callum argued. 'Your father would never want you to sacrifice yourself, and that's what it would be. Giving up your own life for your family?'

'I know,' said Rona miserably. 'But they need me, Father and Doug, and. I'm running the shop now Aunt Lizzie's gone. So I can't leave—you do see that, don't you?'

'I don't see it at all,' said Callum. 'But you've got to make a choice. Either you marry me or you stay at home and become a drudge.'

'It's not like that!' Rona flared up. 'I want to help Father —he depends on me.'

'And what about me?'

'That's selfish,' said Rona.

'Oh don't be so goody-goody.' He was angry now. 'You can't really feel anything for me, or you wouldn't take that attitude.'

'Well, that's how I feel,' Rona said.

'That's your decision,' he said coldly.

'We're quarrelling already,' said Rona, with a little tremor in her voice. 'Oh, Callum, don't let's quarrel. Please . . .'

170

'I wish you'd think it over,' he said. 'I know I could make you happy.'

'Oh, don't!' said Rona miserably torn. 'I won't change my mind. I can't.'

A gust of wind swept a few leaves into the shelter.

'You're getting cold,' he said. 'I shouldn't have brought you here.'

He got up and pulled her to her feet.

'Come on, I'll walk you home.'

They were both silent as they walked back through the town. He looked straight ahead. 'If there's not going to be anything between us, I don't see the point of meeting again, do you?'

'I suppose not,' Rona said in a small voice.

'Well,' he said as they reached the gate of Rona's home. 'Goodbye, Rona. And I wish you . . .' he paused, 'every happiness, maybe with someone else.'

'There won't be!' Rona cried out, and then she turned away.

He watched her as she opened the door and went inside. Indoors, Doug was listening to the football results on the wireless and Angus, his slippers on and his spectacles on the end of his nose, was reading the weekly paper.

It was all a very familiar sight.

Angus looked up. 'See and close the door, Rona. There's a draught blowing in.' He glanced at her.

'Have a nice time.'

171

'Yes, thank you.'

Neither Angus nor Doug paid much attention. Neither noticed that her eyes were bright with tears.

'Well, that's it,' Rona told herself 'It's all over.' And she said as cheerfully as she could, 'Anyone want a cup of tea?'

## ERIKA CONFIDES IN RONA

It doesn't feel a bit like spring, Rona thought. Had she made the right decision? She turned the question over and over in her mind, but always she came back to the same conclusion. I couldn't have done anything else. I've got to stay here.

So she tried to forget about her dilemma, and put on a cheerful face, though Angus, who knew her well, was not fooled by this and often looked at her thoughtfully.

This year Rona found little pleasure, as she usually did, in the great sweep of yellow in the park. Normally she enjoyed the lengthening of the days, but now she didn't feel a lifting of the heart. Life was dull and flat and would go on being so.

She tried very hard to share in Nancy's excitement—for Nancy was engaged to the young man she had met at the badminton club, and was full of wedding plans. 'It will be in summer,' she told Rona. 'We're planning for late June. I want my little bridesmaids in soft sweet pea colours—pale pinks and maybe mauve,' her voice drifted off.

Rona smiled and tried not to think about Callum and whether she had made the right decision.

'And what about Erika?' Nancy was intrigued by the newcomer. 'Is she still as silent?'

'No—she's taking lessons in English from Miss Webb. You know her, she taught at the High.'

'I was scared of her,' admitted Nancy.

Rona laughed. 'Oh, her bark was worse than her bite. And she had endless patience.'

Certainly Erika was gradually becoming more fluent. Every morning, while Angus had been laid up, she'd appeared at the shop door and helped with baking the bread and rolls.

Even when he was back at work, she would come in when she was free and shyly offer to help. Once or twice, she had produced Danish pastries and a gateau. When Angus thanked her, she shook her head. 'For me it is a pleasure,' she said. 'I like to bake. In my father's shop . . .' and she broke off.

Rona was no nearer knowing anything about Erika's history. She tried asking Doug, and he said rather brusquely that it was none of her business. She had a feeling that Doug didn't know either, but that it didn't really

173

matter to him either way.

One day when the shop was quiet, Erika appeared at the door and signalled to Rona.

'When you are free,' she said in a whisper, 'can I talk to you?'

Rona looked surprised. 'I'm not busy now,' she said, because the shop was empty.

'What is it?'

'No.' Erika shook her head. 'It's private.'

'Then come round to the house—this evening,' Rona offered.

Erika hesitated. 'Could we speak alone?'

All right. Say the café. I could be there about half-past five.'

'Good. Thank you.'

She was at the café promptly, but Erika was already waiting at a corner table, a cup of tea untouched in front of her. 'You would like tea, coffee?'

'Coffee, please.' Rona took off her coat and sat down opposite Erika. She was concerned to see that the girl had been crying. What on earth could be wrong?

She leaned across the table and laid a hand on Erika's arm. 'Tell me what's wrong?'

Erika fished in her bag and produced an airmail letter. 'I don't know. My English is not good enough.'

'You want me to read it?'

Erika nodded. 'I explain. My brother—he and I came from Vienna. He got a job in London, but he was always in trouble. For a bit he was in prison.' She gave a little sob. 'I love Franz. He is my brother, but he is not good—he steals, he takes money from his firm. When he got out of prison, he went to Australia.'

Rona was troubled. 'So you want me to read this Is it from your brother?'

Erika shook her head. 'No, he does not write much. He did not learn to read and write well. The letter, it is in English. My English is not good. I must know. Is Franz in trouble again? Is he in prison? Why should someone write to me from Australia?'

Rona turned the blue airmail letter over in her hand—she noticed that it had been redirected from London to an address in Dundee and then to Kirkton.

Erika twisted her handkerchief between her fingers. Her coffee was growing cold and she pushed the cup to one side. 'I know you will help me, you will tell me the truth,' she said. 'I felt I could not ask Doug. If it is bad news I will tell him, of course.'

'*Dear Miss Erika,*' read Rona. She skimmed the letter, trying to make sense of the cramped unfamiliar handwriting. Then she read it more slowly. She looked up at Erika.

'Oh tell me, please quickly,' said Erika. 'Franz, is he back in prison?'

Rona smiled at her. 'No, he's doing well. Listen, I'll read it to you.,'

She began. '*Dear Miss Erika. I write on behalf of your brother, Franz. He is anxious I*

175

*should write to you to tell you his news. Franz came to us a year ago. I have a farm in this part of Queensland, and I wanted a strong man to help with the cattle and the horses. It is hard work and long hours and I wanted someone who was not afraid to roll up his sleeves and get down to it. Glad to say, Miss Erika, I found your brother, through an agency.*

*'He told me just lately he had been in trouble with the law back home—that makes no odds to me, long as he's a hard worker. He's a wonder with the animals. In fact, just a few months ago we had a fire in a barn here, and Franz was great—he calmed down the horses. They were in a panic, as you can imagine. My wife likes Franz, too, and cooks big meals for him.*

*Now, Miss Erika, I'm not much of a one for writing letters, but I thought you'd like to know your brother is turning out OK.*

*Yours respectfully,*

*Will Jensen.*

'Oh, there's something written at the bottom,' said Rona. 'Different handwriting. *Herzliche Grusse von Franz.*'

'Oh, *Gott sei Dank.*' Erika's eyes filled with tears. 'He's written in German—*loving greetings from Franz.* He is well. I'd been afraid for him.' She dabbed at her eyes. 'I have been so worried.'

Rona folded the letter and gave it back to Erika.

'It sounds as if he has made a new life,' she

176

said gently. 'You have no need to worry any more.'

'I will write to him,' said Erika, her face lighting up. 'Now I can tell him about Doug and you and your father and my good friends. And now I will work hard at learning English so I can help in the shop sometimes.'

'You've been a great help already,' said Rona. 'And your English is improving all the time.' She paused, wondering if this was the right moment. 'Erika, have you no other family?'

Erika shook her head. 'None. Only Franz.'

'But your parents?' Rona wondered if she was going too far.

'They died—during the war, in a concentration camp,' said Erika. 'Franz and I, we were sent away. We got to Switzerland, kind people cared for us. Then we came to England after the war. We worked. I got a job in a café, Franz worked in a hotel. We had a little room, but we were poor.'

She told the bare facts of her story simply, without any striving for sympathy. But Rona's heart went out to the girl sitting opposite her.

'But now it is all right!' Erika exclaimed. She beamed at Rona.

'You must tell Doug,' said Rona. 'Show him the letter. You could . . .' she paused, 'you could have told him about Franz. He would have understood.' She stopped. Doug could be maddening at times, but he was fair and kind-

177

hearted. She tried to explain this to Erika.

'I thought,' Erika said in a low voice, 'if he knew about Franz, he would give me up. If Franz was in trouble again I would have to go away somewhere else. I would not want Doug to know someone whose brother was,' here her voice broke.

'Oh, no, he's not like that.' It was hard to put into words what Doug was like—he didn't care about anyone's background. He was just Doug, honest and straightforward.

Suddenly she felt a wave of affection for him, and then she realised how lucky she was to have a family. Father, Doug, even Aunt Lizzie who had often been trying, but really cared about the family.

'Well, don't you worry any more,' Rona said. She got up. 'Time I went home. Listen, why don't you come for tea? I'm making a sausage and apple and onion pie. Aunt Lizzie collected recipes, cut them out of the newspapers, all during the war and after, and she passed them on to me. It's very tasty and there's plenty for four. It's all ready to go into the oven. Come on Erika, join us?'

The girl got up, her eyes shining now. 'Thank you. I will be pleased to.'

# TIME MOVES ON

Rona and Erika were becoming good friends. And what a difference in Doug! He was cheerful and full of energy nowadays. Rona liked the protective way he cared for Erika, and she saw the way they looked at each other. 'If only,' she thought, 'someone cared about me like that.'

Then she pulled herself up sharply. Of course, there was lots to look forward to. There was Nancy's wedding, for a start, and it looked as if Doug and Erika would be making their own wedding plans before long.

Now Erika fitted into the routine at the bakery, and helped there in her spare time. Customers would come into the shop and ask for the Danish pastries she produced. Now and then she would decorate a cake and Rona marvelled at her skill and artistry.

'It is nothing,' she would say, but you could tell that she was proud of her efforts.

And Angus? Often Rona would catch him glancing at her as if he was about to speak and then he thought better of it. Now too, he was beginning to come round to new ideas.

She said one day, 'Father, it's time we had a café. When Mr Grey retires you could do something with the space upstairs. Every baker has a café, even in small places round about, there's a tearoom, and in towns like Cupar—look at Elder's. People would come in for soup and rolls in the middle of the day, or afternoon tea.'

He would shake his head and say, 'Lass, you'll be the ruin of me,' but somehow she felt he was coming round to the idea. But Callum. Oh, she tried not to think about him What a life they might have had together! But he would meet someone else and be happy.

She tried to picture his future in Canada, maybe marrying a farmer's daughter who was large and cheerful and competent, and bringing up a large family of boys who would follow in his footsteps whatever business he chose. And small, pretty, fair-haired girls . . .

'Oh, stop it!' she told herself firmly. 'What's the use of torturing yourself with what might happen in the future?'

Sometimes they met in the town and he'd greet her warmly, but they hadn't talked again, not since that night in the shelter. 'And that's an end to it,' she decided, and felt a wave of bitter misery sweep over her.

She thought that she had hidden her feelings, but other people noticed. 'You haven't been listening,' Nancy told her a little reproachfully.

'Yes, I have, honestly,' said Rona, trying to summon up interest in her friend's account of wedding plans.

'I told you already,' said Doug in

exasperation after she'd asked him a second time whether he'd be in for his tea.

And Angus looked at her often, very thoughtfully.

*     *     *

A few days later there was a call from Mr Grey, the solicitor who rented the premises upstairs from the bakery.

'Mr Maclaren,' he said. 'I'd like a word. Would it be convenient for me to speak to you when you're less busy? Or maybe you could come upstairs?'

'I'll be up in ten minutes.' Angus wiped his hands on a towel. 'Just let me get this batch in the oven.'

He wondered what it could be about. Mr Grey was an ideal tenant—he hoped there was no trouble.

'Good morning, Mr Maclaren.' Miss Mackie, as neat and trim as ever, was at her desk.

She stopped typing and smiled at Angus. 'Mr Grey's expecting you.'

'Good of you to spare the time, Mr Maclaren.' The solicitor came out of his office 'Come away in.'

Angus looked round him at the large roll top desk, the filing cabinets and a few prints of old Kirkton on the walls. This had not changed all the time he could remember. Mr Grey had

181

not changed, either—yes, he had, thought Angus. He was grey-haired now with a slight stoop. How long had they known each other? He tried to recall but he thought with a smile, that they were still on formal terms. It was Mr Maclaren always, not Angus, and Mr Grey, not John.

'Take a seat, Mr Maclaren,' said the lawyer, gesturing towards the comfortable leather chair kept for visitors.

'I hope there's not a problem?' Angus was a little anxious.

'No, no,' Mr Grey reassured him. 'It's just that . . . well, I'm retiring. In six months' time, and I wanted to give you due notice that I'm giving up the lease.'

'Well, now.' Angus didn't quite know what to say. He had thought somehow that the present situation would continue for many years.

'I'm sorry to hear that. No,' he paused. 'No health problems, I hope?'

'Nothing of the kind,' Grey said. 'No, it's just I'm past retiring age and I thought it's time to take life that bit easier. We've a wee cottage up near Aberfeldy and I'm keen on fishing. I'd like fine to have a bit more time to myself.'

Angus felt a little envious, but only for a moment. Then he told himself, he didn't care for fishing and he'd no real hobbies. The bakery was his whole life, his only interest.

What would he do with retirement? It was different for Grey—he still couldn't think of him as John. With his fresh, open-air complexion and sharp eyes, the solicitor seemed well suited to an outdoor life.

'We'll miss you.'

'Likewise,' said Grey. 'You've been the ideal landlord, Angus, if I may be more personal.'

'And what about Miss Mackie?' Angus asked. 'What about the practice?'

'It's being taken over by Wilson's,' said the solicitor. 'Wilson and Grey, it'll be.'

Angus knew the name well—a large firm of solicitors on the other side of the town.

'So Miss Mackie will be going there, and they'll be very glad to have her. She's a fine secretary, efficient, discreet, you couldn't ask for anyone better.'

'So you'll be ending the lease?'

'At the term,' said Grey. 'I have all the papers here. I think you'll find everything in order.'

'I'm sure I will,' said Angus warmly. 'Well, I'll wish you all the very best in your retirement.' He rose and they shook hands. 'A very wise decision. Good luck, John.'

# UPSETTING NEWS FOR RONAN

No-one quite knew how the news about Callum got round the town. But it was true—everyone said so.

'What's that lad of yours going to do now the farm's sold?' Agnes, who helped Callum's mother in the house, was a forthright sort of person.

Callum's mother shook her head. 'Well may you ask,' she said. 'He's talking about going to Canada. We've a cousin not far from Montreal. He's always on at Callum to go out there, but we'll see.'

Agnes was quick to pass on this piece of information to her friend, Jessie, when they met at the social club one evening.

'That laddie, mind, we thought he was courting the baker's lass. He's likely to be going out to Canada to work for a cousin there.'

'Is that so?' said her friend. 'When's he going?'

'I'm not sure,' said Agnes. 'I didna like to be nosey, but it'll be soon from the way his mother spoke.'

Jessie liked a bit of gossip, so she passed on the information. By that time the story had grown. Callum was definitely going—he'd been across in Dundee to book his passage.

Someone had seen him, and yes, it was all off with the baker's daughter. A pity, said some folk. She was a bit harum-scarum still, but a nice lass for all that.

The rumours spread and the news reached Angus as he stood in a queue at the bank.

'So how's the family?' asked an old friend, greeting Angus.

'All grand, thank you.' Angus replied. Though it wasn't quite true. Rona was down in the dumps these days—he could well imagine why.

'She's doing a grand job in the shop,' said his friend, who had a soft spot for Rona. 'I've seen her sometimes with the lad from Harefield Farm, but I hear he's going out to Canada—got a job there. Next week he's sailing, so they tell me.'

'Next week, eh?' said Angus thoughtfully.

\*     \*     \*

He told Rona and Doug as they sat at the table, finishing off second helpings of an apple dumpling.

'I hear that Callum's going off to Canada soon,' he said. 'George Young was telling me—I met him in the bank today. He says the lad's away very shortly. Got his passage all booked.'

'Is that right?' Rona looked up sharply.

'Well, that's what I was told,' Angus said,

185

laying down his spoon. 'That was grand. No-one makes a dumpling like you, Rona.'

'Yes, well, that's maybe all I'm good for,' said Rona sharply. Angus and Doug stared at her. This was so unlike Rona. What had got into her?

'Come on now,' said Angus in a gentle tone.

But Rona suddenly got up, flung down her table napkin and rushed upstairs.

'What's all that about?' Doug looked puzzled. 'Is she not well or something?'

'I've an idea,' said Angus, suddenly understanding.

Doug shook his head, not knowing what was the matter. 'I'll do the dishes, then,' he said getting up.

A little later, Rona appeared. Her eyes were red, and she gave a weak little smile. 'Sorry about that,' she said. 'Now I'll get on with the dishes.'

'Doug's done the washing up,' said her father. 'There's tea in the pot. You sit down, lass.'

'Doug washing up?' Rona said. 'I can't believe it.'

'He's gone out to see that lass of his.' Angus looked at his daughter. 'Are you not going out yourself? Not to meet that young man?'

'He's not my young man.' Rona's voice trembled. She sat down by the fireside and picked up her sewing.

Angus opened the newspaper and scanned

186

the headlines, but he was not concentrating, only trying to decide what he should say to Rona.

'Oh, well,' he began, 'that's a pity now.' He was silent for a bit then he said all of a sudden, 'There's going to be changes—with Mr Grey retiring. I'd thought—and it's all depending on what you feel—of bringing Erika into the business. She knows all about the bakery, and she's got a nice manner with the customers.'

'A good idea,' said Rona warmly. She liked Erika and they'd worked well together.

'And,' Angus added, 'you've been on at me to start a café—well, with John Grey retiring, there's all that space upstairs. I'd have to find a cook, a professional cook who was used to catering.'

'That's a great idea!' said Rona.

'So Maclaren's is expanding—a shop manager, a cook, and maybe if Doug decides to give up the garage, he'll agree to be in charge of the vans.'

'And,' said Rona in a small voice, 'what about me?'

'That's what I'm trying to say.' Angus looked across at her. 'You've done a grand job—taking over the house and the shop when your Aunt Lizzie left. But,' he said slowly, 'I don't want you to feel that Maclaren's has to be your whole life. You might want to go away—you've been talking about London long enough. You might want to get married.'

'That's not likely,' Rona said, and there was a catch in her voice.

'You're a bonny lass,' he said fondly. 'There's many a one would jump at the chance of a wife like you.'

'I don't see them jumping,' said Rona.

'What I'm trying to say,' Angus went on as if she hadn't spoken, 'is that you're not to sacrifice your life to us, to the bakery. There's plenty out there you could be doing. I don't want you to feel one day, that you could have had a better life away from Kirkton.'

He added, looking into the fire, 'Oh, I've enjoyed the bakery, working there, building up the business, but I always had a fancy to travel. Too late now. Though I'd have liked to join the Navy. Still, there was a place in the bakery—and old Mr Simpson gave me a good training. I was glad to take over when he went, but, all the same . . .' his voice died away.

Then he said, quite fiercely, 'I don't want you to give up anything. It's only a business when all's said and done. Not worth ruining your life for, and it isn't as if we were going downhill. Far from it. I've great plans,' he said more briskly.

'Well, I'll remember that,' said Rona. 'Though I've no plans myself at the moment,' she said a little bleakly.

'Well, there's always folk on the move,' said Angus. 'Time was; you had to stay where you were born and brought up, and no chance to see the world. Speaking of seeing the world,' he added, turning back to the newspaper, 'there's Callum away to Canada next week, George told me.'

Rona laid down her sewing. 'Excuse me.' She got up from her chair and ran upstairs.

Angus looked after in surprise. What could be the matter? Was it the news about young Callum going to Canada?

He shook his head. You could never tell with a lassie, what she was thinking.

## A FINAL CHANCE

Rona ran down the road to the phone box. Luckily it was empty. She picked up the phone with a shaky hand. What if he wasn't there? What if he didn't want to speak to her? What if—oh, what if he had already gone? But she had to know.

'Harefield Farm,' she recognised the warm friendly tones of Callum's mother.

'I wondered,' she hesitated, 'if I could have a word with Callum.'

'Oh, it's you, Rona—just you wait a minute. I think he's about.'

She could hear sounds in the background, the wireless switched off, and Callum's mother calling, 'It's for you, Callum—she's in a phone box so hurry up.'

'Rona?' Callum sounded surprised. 'Is something wrong?'

'No, nothing.' She paused. 'It was just that I wanted to see you—only for a few minutes to—'

He interrupted her. 'Yes, sure. Say, at the café? Tonight? Seven o'clock, maybe?'

'Thank you.'

'I have to go,' he said rather abruptly.

She put the phone down, trembling a little Had she made a big mistake? Had he already pushed her into a corner of his mind as someone he'd once known and would forget?

She was there at the café a little early, but Callum was on time. She watched him coming along the road towards her, with that long, swinging stride she remembered so well.

'Rona! I haven't kept you waiting?'

'No, I'm just here,' she said quickly.

'Right. A cup of coffee?'

'If you don't mind—maybe we could just go for a walk.'

'Sure,' he said easily. 'Come on, we'll walk along the front.'

They strolled in silence for a bit, then stopped to watch the few people walking dogs along the beach and smiled at a large black Labrador leaping into the waves. It was a warm early summer evening with the promise of sunny days to come.

'So?' Callum turned to Rona as they reached the shelter where they'd sat often.

190

'Was there something special you wanted to see me about?' His tone was neutral.

Rona gulped. 'Just to say goodbye and to wish you good luck, before you sail next week,'

He looked puzned. 'Sail? Next week?'

'For Canada. I know you'd planned to go—to join your cousin.'

'But . . .' he was even more confused. 'I'm not sailing next week, probably not for a month or so yet. I've only just made enquiries about the passage. What on earth gave you that idea?'

'My father said . . .' Rona stared at him. 'My father said just last night, that you were sailing in a few days' time. He was quite definite. He'd met someone in the bank who said you were leaving next week. Seems it's common knowledge.'

'Rona.' Callum took her hands in his. 'I don't know how these rumours get around. Oh, yes I do,' he said, realising. 'I met someone I knew on the ferry just after I'd been to the travel agent's in Dundee. We were taking about possibly emigrating. Do you think,' he said thoughtfully, 'that your father's trying to push us together? Come to think of it, he was talking about the future of the bakery. How Erika's going to join the business and Doug will take over the vans. Oh, and he's planning to open a tearoom upstairs when the lawyer's lease runs out. I wonder . . .'

She blushed. 'This is very embarrassing. I'd

191

never have rung you if I'd realised, but I didn't want you to go without saying goodbye.'

'I'm glad you rang. So,' Callum said slowly, 'there's going to be changes. But you'll be staying in Kirkton?'

'Father said,' Rona drew a deep breath, 'that I'd to do just what I wanted. When he was young he'd given up a plan to join the Navy and got a job in the bakery instead. He wanted me to have the freedom to choose, to go wherever I wanted. London, maybe.' Her voice trailed off.

'Or Canada?' said Callum, looking into her eyes. 'Canada with me? Would you, Rona? You said that you couldn't leave your family, but it seems things are going to change at the bakery. So,' he added, 'have you given up plans to go to London, get a glamorous job or,' he paused, 'Rona, would you think of coming to Canada with me? What I'm saying is, would you marry me?'

'Oh, yes!' Rona's face lit up with joy. 'Yes!'

'Wheeh!' Callum leapt up and waved his fists in the air.

'I couldn't forget you,' he said as he put his arms around her. 'But I didn't think there was any hope for me.'

'And I thought,' Rona said a little shakily, 'that you'd go to Canada and meet someone else. I had an idea she'd be a farmer's daughter and you'd have three boys, all tall and good looking and maybe a couple of little girls—

192

very pretty, fair-haired girls.'

'You'd got it all planned, hadn't you?' He smiled at her. 'I'd rather have you.' He went on, 'I'm not the romantic sort—no good at making pretty speeches, but well, you're the only one for me.'

He kissed her and Rona felt as if they were the only ones on earth, two people in love.

'What a way to behave!' Two elderly women were passing the shelter. One glared at Callum who took no notice.

'Och,' said her companion, who was little and round and good-natured. 'Where's the harm in having a kiss and a cuddle in a shelter?' She thought a little wistfully of the young man who many years ago had kissed her in a seaside shelter.

'Well,' said the other, 'my feet are hurting me. I wanted to sit down for a bit.'

The other sighed. 'We'll find somewhere else to sit and maybe go and have an ice-cream or a nice cup of tea in the town.'

She wondered about the young couple. Were they engaged, perhaps? She hoped they were and that they'd have a long and happy life together. There was nothing, she thought, quite like a bit of romance.

'Do hurry up,' said her friend crossly. 'I'm dying for a cup of tea and a nice sit down.'

The first woman sighed. All right, dear.' She turned back along the promenade, but the thought of the romantic scene she'd left behind gave her a glow. Someone else's happiness, that was the next best thing.

*    *    *

'It's got to be the best ever,' said Angus to Erika. 'I'll need to Leave the decorating to you.'

'You may be sure,' said Erika solemnly, 'that it will be the very best I can do.'

He smiled at her. More and more Angus was coming to rely on Erika. She was dependable, and now that Rona was going away Erika would be a tower of strength in the shop.

He would miss Rona sadly. In the weeks before the wedding and her departure with Callum for Canada, he tried not to think of what life would be like without her, but then she couldn't have found a better husband than Callum.

He was a good lad and he'd look after Rona. And it might not have all come about. It must have been a rumour, all that story about Callum leaving for Canada, booked his passage, sailing the next week.

That was Kirkton for you. A typical small town.

He'd been a bit surprised when Callum came to ask—as was very right and proper—for Angus's permission to marry Rona. 'I'm not actually planning to go to Canada for a couple of months,' Callum explained. 'So there's time to book our passage and we can get married before I go.'

He looked at Angus with a twinkle in his eye, and Angus wondered just how much the lad knew about the rumour that had gone round the town.

Neither he nor Rona had ever said anything. But his daughter was a different girl now. She sang around the house, and chattered about their plans. 'And Erika will look after you well, Father,' she said.

'It's just to be a quiet wedding,' said Callum. 'That's what we want. Only family.'

Aunt Lizzie came down from Perth on the bus, and was about to take charge. 'It's all planned, Auntie,' said Rona. 'Just a quiet ceremony and a family lunch.'

'No show of presents! No bridesmaids!'

Rona shook her head. 'It's all going to be very simple. Just family and a few friends.'

Friends such as Nancy, who was thrilled by Rona's news. It was not long after her own wedding and, 'I knew you'd be next!' she beamed.

'But a wedding cake, that you must have,' said Angus, 'and the very best that Maclaren's Bakery can provide.'

And of course, it had to have pride of place in the window. Angus cleared the window completely of the tins of shortbread and display of fruit cakes. 'You'll need to arrange the display,' he said anxiously to Erika.

'Leave it to me,' she smiled at him.

On a base of cream silky material, at either side of the window stood an arrangement in a silver container of white roses and maidenhair fern. And in the centre stood the cake—a three-tier, rich fruit cake decorated with all Erika's skill and artistry, with piped shells and lattice work and sugar roses.

People stopped to look into the window. 'My, that's braw!' said one elderly woman.

'Who's getting married then?'

'Do you not know—it's the baker's lassie. She marrying Callum Scott and they're away to Canada.'

'It's a grand cake,' said her friend as they moved away up the street.

Rona had overheard the conversation and she suddenly felt in the midst of all the excitement and anticipation, a great wave of love for all those she was leaving behind.

For Father, for Doug and Erika, for Nancy and her friends—for Aunt Lizzie too. And she knew that however far away she might be— over thousands of miles and a vast ocean—she would still be the baker's lassie.